THE PRESIDENT IS MISSING

A Matt Blake Novel

Russell F. Moran

The President is Missing
Coddington Press

Copyright © 2017 by Russell F. Moran
Printed in the United States of America

ISBN 0996346694
ISBN 13: 9780996346696

Cover Design by Erin Kelly
http://erinkelly.webs.com/

This book is a work of fiction. The characters, names, incidents, dialogue and plot are
the products of the author's imagination or are used fictitiously. Any resemblance to
actual persons or events is purely coincidental.
www.morancom.com

DEDICATION

This book is dedicated to the United States Navy SEALs.

ACKNOWLEDGEMENTS

As always, I thank my wife, Lynda, for her attentive reading and rereading of my many drafts, and for laughing at my jokes. I also thank my friend and copy editor, John White, for his proofreading and editing. And I especially thank my readers, many of whom are a constant source of inspiration and encouragement for me.

AUTHOR'S NOTE

You will find a **Cast of Characters** after the last chapter of the book. It can be frustrating to come across a character on page 150, who you first met on page 20, especially if you've put the book down for a few days. I've seen this done in Russian literature, and I happily add a cast of characters to *The President is Missing*, as well as my other novels.

CHAPTER 1

"What the hell just happened?" I asked Barbara Hightower, my assistant.

We were watching a TV first, a live broadcast by the President of the United States from a nuclear submarine deep under the waters of the South Atlantic. The President, Matt Blake, also happens to be my husband. Matt, dressed in naval officer's fatigues, faced the camera holding a microphone. He looked great, but then he always does. Matt's so natural in front of a camera, it's as if the technology was invented for him. But the screen suddenly went blank.

"Beats me, ma'am," Barbara said. "If we can't maintain communications with a nuclear submarine, what the hell can we communicate with?"

A TV anchorman just appeared on the screen.

"This is Shepard Smith for FOX News, ladies and gentlemen. If you were watching you just saw that our communications link with the *USS Louisiana* went blank. This is an odd situation, because the communications links between the shore and our nuclear ballistic missile submarine fleet is the most sophisticated available.

The *USS Louisiana* is the latest and probably the last of the Ohio Class nuclear ballistic missile submarines. There are 18 Ohio Class subs in service, including 14 ballistic missile submarines, and four cruise missile subs. The ballistic missile subs, such as the *Louisiana*, carry 16 nuclear missiles. At 560 feet in length, she displaces almost 17,000 tons. The president was addressing the nation from the sub's control room and discussing the recent renovation of the huge vessel when we lost communications. We will continue the live feed as soon as it's been reestablished."

"Hey, they've never done a live TV network feed from under the ocean before," I said. "Maybe the technology just has to shake out a bit. I remember Matt giving a speech before the United Nations once, when his sound blanked out. There he was in a gigantic auditorium with his lips moving but no sound coming out. He shouted 'Read my lips' to laughs and applause. Right after that the sound came back on. Matt's good at handling awkward situations. Our contact with the sub should be back on in a minute."

I was trying to cheer myself up and calm down at the same time. Can you imagine seeing your husband on TV when suddenly he disappears?

Five minutes went by, then ten. Still no communication with the sub. Small talk with Barbara was doing nothing for my twisting stomach. I looked at the TV remote in my hand. A remote is a pretty amazing invention when you think about it. Without moving you just point it at the TV and see a lengthy guide, click one of the buttons and see the details of a movie, click another button and control sound, save and rewind, or turn the TV on and off. But Matt just cut out and I can't press a button on this worthless piece of shit to bring him back. I shared all of these thoughts with Barbara. The look on her face told me what I suspected, that I was starting to rant like a fucking lunatic.

The intercom buzzed from the receptionist's desk. I stood up from my spot on the couch and ran across the room, suddenly feeling like an idiot. Barbara's not just an assistant, she's a good friend, and she's great at putting up with my changing moods. I spoke into the receiver but didn't hear a response on the other end. That's because I was holding it upside down. Barbara gently took the receiver out of my hand and answered, "Office of the First Lady, may I help you." She handed the receiver to me—right side up.

"Ma'am, it's Admiral Patterson, Chief of Naval Operations, on the phone for you," said the duty officer at NavOps.

Oh Dear God, I thought. Why would Ashley be calling me? Ashley Patterson and I are good friends. I've seen her naval career skyrocket over the years, because of one reason—she's a smart, tough military leader. At the age of 40, Ashley is a tall, beautiful black woman, a rising star in the Navy. When Ashley speaks, people listen, not because of the military timbre in her voice, but because you realize that you're talking to a leader. She's one of the best commanders we have in the military.

But why the hell would the CNO be calling me out of the blue? Asking myself stupid questions somehow made me feel better.

"Dee (we're too close for her to call me Madam First Lady), I'm about to be interviewed by Fox News. This isn't good, hon. We've received reports of an underwater explosion near the coordinates of the *Louisiana's* last position. Reports of debris are coming in. Dee, I'm afraid that the sub, along with your husband, may have been lost."

"I'll be there in 10 minutes, Ashley," I said. The Pentagon is just over three miles from the White House, so getting there in 10 minutes wasn't a problem, barring a traffic jam.

When my car pulled up to the Pentagon, a Marine guard, plus my normal Secret Service detail, escorted Barbara and me to the operations room. I felt like my brain was shutting down, but I refused to let it happen. Matt Blake, the President of the United States, isn't just my husband. He's my lover, my confidant, my best friend. He's the most important person in my life. Could he be dead? Matt occupies such a huge part of my reality that the idea of his death wasn't ringing true to me. I think psychologists call it cognitive dissonance. It's the stress you feel when you try to hold two competing thoughts in your mind at the same time. Matt's just fine, I thought. I had a crisp picture of him in my head. But, and here's the dissonance part, the Chief of Naval Operations has just told me that he may have died. I guess any couple who are close and in love have a hard time accepting the idea that their spouse may be dead. But my friend Ashley seemed to think Matt was gone along with the sub. I need to look at the evidence before I'm ready to make any conclusions. When Matt practiced law, he was one of the best trial lawyers in the country. I should know—I worked on all of his cases, not as a dutiful help mate, but because I found his work fascinating. One thing that Matt drilled into my head was to look at the evidence—all of it—and then *distrust* the evidence.

We walked into the operations room as Ashley was making a statement for TV. The broadcast was carried over all of the TV and cable networks.

"I have a startling development to report this morning," Ashley said after she was introduced by her deputy. "At 10:45 a.m.—25 minutes ago—we lost all communications with the nuclear submarine *USS Louisiana*. President Blake was addressing the nation from the sub when our link was broken. We've received reports, confirmed by listening devices, that there was an explosion near the last known location of the *Louisiana*. Prior to the explosion, the sub made a sudden hard turn. We have no idea why, but it's possible that the captain of the sub was maneuvering to avoid a torpedo. Aerial reconnaissance confirmed a large debris field in the area. I'm not going to speculate, ladies and gentlemen. I've given you the facts as we know them, and my office will keep the nation briefed as any new information comes in."

Ashley walked over to me. She abandoned protocol and hugged me. She held me by the shoulders and looked into my eyes.

"Dee, I'm sorry my friend. It doesn't look good."

It doesn't look good. That's a polite way of saying that your husband may be splattered all over the South Atlantic. We can't control our thoughts, just as we can't control the shit that life sometimes throws at us. I thought about the White House, and the possibility that Matt might not be coming home.

Life in the White House isn't easy to describe. Countless articles and books have been written on the subject over the years, ever since George Washington occupied the office. Every president since John Adams has lived at 1600 Pennsylvania Avenue. That means the place has been occupied by a President of the United States since 1800. The mansion was set afire by the British during the War of 1812. While the White House was still under reconstruction, President James Monroe moved in, and construction resumed. The semi-circular South Portico was finished in 1824, and the North Portico in 1829. Although the residence had expanded in size, it became cramped because it was also the site of endless government and ceremonial functions. In 1900, President Theodore Roosevelt ordered all office space to be relocated to the West Wing. He also gave the residence its official name, the White House, although it was common for people to refer to the place by that name before it became official. It had been known over the years by various names, including the "President's Palace," the "President's House," and the "Executive Mansion." Eight years after

Roosevelt, President Taft expanded the West Wing and added the Oval Office. The place drips history. Both Matt and I are history buffs, and we never get over the feeling of awe, but, typical of Matt, he insisted that he and I look at it as a home, not just an official residence. Not easy. We both feel that life in the White House adds a deep dimension to our lives.

But now he's missing. I may be packing my bags soon.

CHAPTER 2

I just experienced the weirdest sensation of my life. As I stood in the control room of the *USS Louisiana* giving my address to the nation, the sub suddenly took a nose dive. I'm not familiar with submarine movements, but that's the only way I can describe it—a nose dive. As the sub pulled out of its dive I felt the strongest g-force I'd ever experienced. When I trained for the Recon Marines, we were flown to a high altitude in an airplane which would then suddenly turn into a deep dive. When the plane pulled out of the plunge, the feeling was like having your body pressed into the deck. That's the only feeling like the one I just experienced. I fell to the deck, my legs unable to support me. Then the sub leveled off and accelerated, pushing me across the deck into a bulkhead. I wasn't accustomed to the sightless orientation of a sub, and could only go by the feelings my body gave off. There are no portholes to look through to see what's happening. Then I heard a loud explosion from behind and I felt the sub shudder.

The captain was standing nearby, holding onto a rail. He didn't look upset, or even surprised.

I stood up, my legs still trembling, and grabbed a rail to steady myself. I could hear the sound of distant gunfire, amplified by the confines of a submarine.

"Captain, can you explain what just happened?"

"Certainly, Mr. President, but there's a gentleman here who can explain it better than me."

A man walked into the control room. He was a bit short, maybe 5'8," and overweight. He wore the uniform of a Russian Naval officer. A *Russian* Naval Officer?

"Good morning, Mr. President. My name is Vasili Yuschenko. I'm an admiral in the Russian Navy. Please do not be concerned. You are perfectly safe, as is Mr. Riordan, your chief of staff."

"I'm waiting for an explanation, Admiral," I said.

"I'm known as a blunt man, Mr. President, so that's exactly how I shall address your question. Russia has captured the *USS Louisiana* and you are now our prisoner and our hostage. That explosion you heard was a ruse, a contrived event to make the world think that the *Louisiana* has been destroyed. You are being taken to a location that I'm not yet ready to disclose."

"What happened to the crew?" I asked. "What about my Secret Service detail?"

"Mr. President, we had to take some drastic steps, as I'm sure you understand. Your people put up a brave struggle. Some of the crew have been shot, along with your personal body guards from your Secret Service. A few remain as prisoners."

"Did you personally order the killings?" I asked.

"No, but I stand behind the actions of my men."

He looked down at the deck when he said that. He looked like a guy who was reporting something that he'd rather not talk about.

"Pardon me for being a skeptic, Admiral, but are you saying that you're holding me, the President of the United States, as a hostage? Are you going to try to arrange for a prisoner exchange? Has Vladimir Putin lost his mind?"

"Putin has lost more than his mind, Mr. President. He has lost his power. Exactly three hours ago a new regime took the reins of power in Russia by a coup d'état. Our new president is Boris Chernekov. I'm sure you're familiar with his name."

"Yes, I'm quite familiar with it." I said.

Time to shut up, I thought. Do not give this man your opinion that Chernekov is a psychopathic madman who wants nothing more than world domination.

"What about the crew of the *Louisiana*?" I said. "Are they part of a mutiny?"

"Yes, Mr. President, some of them are definitely mutineers. The others have been shot. You are going through a carefully planned and executed operation. We've been working on this for years. For Vladimir Putin, it was just a contingency exercise. Boris Chernekov decided to make it a reality, and he planned it to coincide with the coup against Putin. When we heard the announcement that you would be visiting the *Louisiana*, we knew it was time to act. As far as the world is concerned, the *Louisiana* is missing, and so are you."

So the world thinks I'm dead. Dee thinks I'm dead. It's a sickening feeling when you know that the person you love has the wrong information about you—and there's not a goddam thing you can do about it. You can't call and say you're alright. You can't text or email her. You just have to accept the fact that your wife thinks you're dead. I focused my attention back to the admiral.

"Is the *Louisiana's* captain, Joseph Campbell, part of the mutiny?" I asked.

"Yes, he is, a valuable part."

It was hard to believe what I just heard. Captain Joseph Campbell is a well-known officer in the Navy. A Naval Academy graduate, his many assignments included Naval Aide to the White House under my predecessor. Campbell is about six feet in height and he looks the part of a disciplined military leader. He was on a lot of short lists, including mine, to make admiral. Now he's part of a mutiny? I pride myself on judging a person's character, a trait that helped get me into the White House. But Campbell fooled a lot of people, including me. We were totally ignorant of who he really was. A solid character you thought you could count on turns out to be a treasonous son of a bitch.

"What do you want from me?" I said.

"I want you to be comfortable and worry free. Your next role in our operation will be disclosed to you in time, and not by me. Actually, I don't know what your future role will be. My aide will now show you to your quarters, and I trust you will find them comfortable. You will be guarded by armed personnel at all times, so I suggest that you abandon any fantasies as a former Marine war hero."

CHAPTER 3

"Admiral Patterson is waiting to see you, Madam First Lady," Ashley's aide said.

My mind, which I haven't quite lost yet, is racing. I'm sitting in the Naval Operations Room at the Pentagon with Admiral Ashley Patterson for another meeting. We're waiting for Admiral Peter Spratt, the Commander of Submarine Forces, United States Navy. While Ashley brought me up to date on the latest information, I kept myself busy shredding a napkin.

FLOTUS is a strange word if you think about it. The word makes me think about garbage floating on the water. Sorry, I know that's gross, but I can't control my hidden thoughts.

FLOTUS, of course, is an acronym for First Lady of the United States. That's who I am. I take back what I said about the garbage.

My Secret Service code name is "Tweetie." I guess I got the name because I'm a big Twitter user. The code name is assigned by the White House Communications Agency, not the Secret Service

11

as many people believe. The code names were once secret, but no more. They're now chosen for brevity, clarity, and tradition. The first letter is always the same for the President and the First Lady. My husband's codename is "Tango." They named him that because he's a good dancer. I guess if he made people laugh all the time they would have called him "Pisser." Matt's also known as POTUS for President of the United States.

So here I am with a PhD from the University of Chicago, eight books published, plus countless articles and papers, and I'm known as Tweetie the FLOTUS.

My real name is Diana Blake, or Dee as those close to me say, and I'm married to Matthew Blake, the President of the United States, the man I love, the man who went missing an hour ago.

As we waited for Admiral Spratt I kept trying to keep myself from passing out. The most important person in my life is missing, possibly dead, and here I am in yet another fucking meeting.

Spratt walked in and took his seat at the conference table. At one end of the table was a large video screen.

"You may find this upsetting, Dee," Ashley said. "It shows the debris field near the last known location of the *Louisiana*."

I grabbed the leg of the table to stop my hand from shaking. If I had a stronger grip I think I would have splintered the thing.

The video was more than upsetting. It was confusing. Splayed across the screen were countless white objects with printing on them. There must have been a hundred or more.

Distrust the evidence—*always* distrust the evidence.

"What are those objects?" I asked.

"Flotation devices of various types, including life rings and standard flotation vests," Admiral Spratt said.

"Can you zoom in on a couple of them?" I asked.

The camera panned in on one flotation device after another. All of them bore the inscription *USS Louisiana.*

"I have some questions," I said.

The admiral didn't know that I already had the answers. I'm an obsessive compulsive when it comes to research, and I always found submarines fascinating – a vessel surrounded by a sheet of metal deep under water. To add to its mystery, a submarine is referred to as a "boat," never a ship. When Matt planned his underwater address to the nation, I plunged into everything there was to read about submarines, and I thoroughly briefed Matt before his trip. But I wanted to hear what the admiral had to say.

"Well, ma'am," Spratt said, "we won't know conclusively until we recover the data recorder, but the sailing plan called for the sub to be in 1,000 feet of water at the time."

"But if the implosion was the result of water pressure, it would have been much deeper, yes?" I said. "Since we get reports steadily from the data recorder, wouldn't it have alerted us to something out of the ordinary?"

"Yes, ma'am, we should have been alerted."

"And what is the maximum depth a sub can go before it's crushed?"

"Anything over about 2,400 feet would result in crushing water pressure," Spratt said.

"Can you describe for me what happens when a submarine is crushed, admiral?"

I already knew the ugly answer, but I wanted to hear it from Spratt.

"First, the hull is crushed, then all of the interior bulkheads are pushed inward. Think of an aluminum can run over by a steam roller."

"Another question, Admiral," I said. "Where are life preservers and other flotation devices stowed on the sub? Are they in lockers or lying around the walkways?"

"The vast majority of life preservers would have been in lockers, ma'am. They would be broken out for distribution on orders from the officer of the deck in response to an emergency."

"One more question," I said, "and then I have some observations. Can you tell me how long it was between the explosion and the appearance of debris on the surface?"

"As best as we can tell, ma'am, it was five minutes until the first pieces of debris appeared."

It was time for me to brief the admiral on the ways of evidence.

"When I worked on legal cases with my husband, he always told me to completely examine the evidence, and then *don't trust the evidence.* I don't know about you two, but I do not trust the evidence we're looking at. From what Admiral Spratt just said, a sub gets crushed when the water pressure collapses its hull. So please answer this question for me: How the hell can all of those hundreds of life preservers have made their way out from behind twisted metal and bubble to the surface in five minutes?"

"What's your thinking, Dee?" Ashley asked.

"My thinking is that the evidence we're looking at is pure bullshit. I'm going to make a naked assertion and say that this evidence was planted. It was manufactured. The debris didn't come from the *Louisiana,* but from some other source."

"But what would have happened to the *Louisiana?*" Spratt asked.

"I think it was hijacked—stolen," I said. "It was either a mutiny or a hijacking. I believe that the *Louisiana* still exists, but God knows where. POTUS is alive I'm telling you. Matt is now a hostage."

I realized that I had just crossed a line. I went from being respected First Lady to hysterical wife in a few moments. "Distrust the evidence," Matt always said. That's what I'm doing.

"Dee Blake is one of the smartest people I've ever met," Ashley said. "What she pointed out here this morning has got me thinking. I can't find anything implausible about what she's said. I agree that the debris came to the surface awfully fast. How about you, Pete?"

"The idea of an American nuclear sub being stolen is a bit far-fetched by my thinking," Spratt said, "but the First Lady's observations about the depth and the debris field are right on. Mrs. Blake has a reputation for thinking outside the box, and we just saw it on display. Admiral Patterson, I recommend that we investigate the possibility that the *Louisiana* was hijacked with a fake explosion in the background."

⇒⊹ ⊹⇐

"I just got a text from Vice-president Roland Benton," I said. "He's going to be sworn in as acting president under the 25th Amendment this afternoon and wants me to be there. Rolly is a good guy. As you know, he's a retired Navy admiral, and once commanded SEAL Team Six. Rolly gets it. I want to talk to him about what we discussed this morning."

My screaming stomach was feeling better. I don't think my theory of a hijacking is the ranting of a hysterical wife. After looking at those bullshit photos of "debris," I think it just may be the truth.

CHAPTER 4

"I do solemnly swear that I will faithfully execute the Office of President of the United States, and will to the best of my ability, preserve, protect, and defend the Constitution of the United States."

Vice-President Roland (Rolly) Benton stood before Chief Justice John Roberts as he recited the oath of office. The swearing in ceremony of the President of the United States is normally one of gigantic crowds and as much pomp and circumstance as our nation can muster. A small army of people are assigned to the event to help with the spectacle. But, as is always the case with the death of a president (I hate to even *think* those words), this ceremony was small and brief. Think about the photo of Lyndon Johnson standing next to Jackie Kennedy on Air Force One taking the oath of office after President Kennedy was assassinated.

The swearing in of Roland Benton took place in the Oval Office with only 25 people present. Because of the circumstances, his oath was not followed by thunderous applause and cheers, only polite clapping. The atmosphere of the room can only be described as uncomfortable. I think people felt uptight because I was there. Tough shit, I thought. Nobody's more uncomfortable than me.

"My fellow Americans. I have just taken the oath of office as *acting* President of the United States. Until we receive definitive proof, we're operating under the assumption that President Blake is alive, and will address ourselves to that question with everything in our power. Our nation has received a shock to its very soul. May God bless America."

Rolly Benton is a good man. Matt couldn't have picked a better running mate. He and Rolly are also good friends. In the three short months of Matt's administration, I noticed that Rolly was the perfect team player. At age 58, he's an excellent public speaker, although nowhere close to Matt. He's a good-looking guy, 5'11', with light sandy colored blond hair and brown eyes. As a retired admiral and former commander of Navy SEAL Team Six, Rolly has a reputation as a man who gets things done, without any bullshit. His wife passed away from cancer two years ago, so the White House will be without a First Lady. After his swearing-in ceremony and his brief address, he asked me to join him for a private chat.

"In my career, Dee, I've been in many painful situations, but this one tops them all. You and Matt had, I mean have, a relationship like a page out of literature. Before we get into substantive issues, I want to ask you a stupid question. How are you bearing up under all this?"

"Mr. President…"

"The name's Rolly."

"Sorry, Rolly. If you don't mind, I'd like to ask you a preliminary question. Am I behaving like a crazy bitch? Am I acting like the hysterical wife who may be a widow but doesn't want to accept it?"

"No, you're not, Dee. You're behaving like the woman we've all grown to like and trust. You're one of the smartest and emotionally solid people I've ever known. The way I size it up, your brain is in full control of your emotions. So let me repeat my question, how are you bearing up?"

"It isn't easy, Rolly. As you know, Matt and I had—have—a relationship that I think is rare. The thought that he may be dead is gripping me like a python. *But,* I don't think he's dead. Have you been briefed by Admiral Patterson on my theory that the *Louisiana* may have been hijacked?"

"Yes, she briefed me completely before you got here, Dee. My initial response was that you were just grabbing at straws, but when I listened to the details, I thought you may be on to something. I also got an intelligence briefing this morning that you may find interesting."

He shoved a document across the desk.

"Read it aloud, Dee."

TOP SECRET - FOR THE PRESIDENT'S EYES ONLY
"Underwater listening devices in the South Atlantic have picked up a faint signal from a large underwater craft. The sound signature confirms that it could be an Ohio Class nuclear submarine. It is travelling slowly north northeast with its engines rigged for silence."

Oh, my God. I just saw confirmation that I may not be indulging in hysterics. My theory just may be on target.

"Dee, I've just shared with you the most Top Secret information in the country right now. I've shared this with you not just out of sympathy, but because I trust your thoughts and instincts."

"Thank you, Mr. President...Rolly, whatever. I have no idea what to do next, but I'm sure there's protocol for this. Who do I talk to about relocating? I hope it will only be temporary, but obviously I can't stay here. Whoever is in charge of situations like this, please have him or her contact me on my cell phone. The last thing in the world that I want to do is get in your way of running the country. I've got to start packing my things." It occurred to me that I was babbling like a lunatic.

"Dee, I'm still located at the vice-president's quarters. Don't be in a big rush to do anything. You still live here as far as I'm concerned. I've communicated with your assistant, Barbara, and she's staying in her room near yours. Please see me here at 8 a.m. tomorrow for breakfast. There's a lot I want to talk to you about."

I showed up at the Oval Office at 8 a.m. I'm an early riser so the time was no problem with me. We sat in the small dining room nearby, and I tried to think of a meal that wouldn't upset my already screaming stomach. When the waiter came to us I ordered an English muffin without butter, despite the wonderful menu he handed to me.

"Chef Franco makes great omelets," Rolly said. "Is that all you want?"

"You don't want a half-eaten omelet on this beautiful carpet," I said. "An English muffin will do."

"Dee, let me get right to the point. I want you to take on an official position, not just honored former First Lady. Dee, I want you to be my Chief of Staff."

Holy shit. First, yesterday's intelligence briefing, and now he asks me to take one of the most important positions in his administration. Was he just being polite? That's not like Rolly. He thinks things through and he thinks fast. I was glad I skipped the omelet.

"But how can I be your Chief of Staff?"

"Simple. Just say yes. I'm not asking you to take on a ceremonial title. I'm asking you to be on the inside. Everybody with a connection to the West Wing knew that you and Tony Riordan, Matt's chief of staff, shared the responsibility of serving your president, your husband. It's no secret that Matt wanted you to be Secretary of State. He wanted you to take that job for the same reason I'm asking you to take this one. Dee, you're enormously talented with a mind that never quits. Your primary job is to head up the *Louisiana* investigation. I've appointed Phil Smith as deputy chief of staff. He can take on most of the routine day-to-day details. Nobody could be a better Chief of Staff than you. I'm not saying that to blow smoke, I'm saying that because I've seen you in action, and I want you on my team. Your job is to put me out of my job, and find the President of the United States. Dee, your job is to find your husband."

Events have never moved faster in my life. Just hours ago Matt went missing, and now I'm being asked to take on one of the biggest jobs in Washington. The way Rolly put it—my primary job is to find Matt—made it hard to say no.

"I accept, Mr. President—Rolly. The way you said it makes it impossible to turn the job down. But keep in mind, sir, that I will work for you. I expect you to fire me if you suspect I have another agenda."

"I'm not worried about that, Dee. We have the same agenda. Sure, I feel tremendously honored to be President of the United States, but I only want this job if it really belongs to me. And I have strong suspicions that it doesn't. I think of myself as a caretaker, a place holder until we find Matt. You may be interested to know that I will be sleeping in the Lincoln guest bedroom. I refuse to completely move into the President's quarters."

The position of Chief of Staff to the president is the highest ranking job in the White House, next to president and vice-president. The position is a modern successor to the earlier job entitled the president's private secretary. The role was formalized as assistant to the president in 1946 in the Truman Administration, and acquired its current name when Kennedy was in office in 1961.

The idea of Chief of Staff seems to have taken off in all walks of life. Now, you can find a chief of staff in a Rotary Club, Kiwanis, or a local chamber of commerce. The Chief of Staff to the President of the United States, however, is a powerful one. The Chief of Staff is appointed by and serves at the pleasure of the president. It does not require senate confirmation. I didn't say it, of course, but Rolly has made a wise choice. I've yet to meet anybody who can kick ass as well as me.

⊷⊶

"Dee, your theory that the Louisiana may have been hijacked is brilliant. Admiral Spratt and his staff had some doubts within minutes of the *Louisiana's* disappearance. That yard-sale debris field is absolute bullshit, as you put it. No way could all of those flotation devices surface within five minutes of a sub being crushed under water. When Admiral Spratt and CNO Patterson heard it from you, that nailed it for them. And of course there is the unexplained sudden shift in course and acceleration of the *Louisiana* just before the explosion."

"Any suspicions so far, Mr. President? I'm sorry, but I have a hard time calling you Rolly."

"Yes, we have some strong suspicions, but we have no idea about future intentions. We think it was the Russians. Besides the fact that they're the only ones with the ability to pull something like this off, we also have to take notice of the new regime in Russia. As you've no doubt heard, Boris Chernekov has deposed Vladimir Putin, and has taken the Russian presidency by coup. Chernekov is old school KGB—extremely old school. He makes Putin look like a school crossing guard. Chernekov has made it clear in countless speeches that he wants to restore the old Soviet Union and he's willing to do it by force if necessary. He's a fucking lunatic, if you pardon my language, but a smart one. His whole career is one of taking risks, sometimes crazy risks. You may recall that he tried to convince Putin to replace the Hungarian Prime Minister with one of Russia's choosing. Now that he's president, there's little to stop him. And what could be riskier than to steal an American nuclear submarine and kidnap the President of the United States?"

"What could their strategy be?" I asked, posing a question for Rolly as well as myself. "If they're holding Matt as a prisoner, what is the bargain they're looking for? A friggin' hostage exchange? And what the hell are they going to do with one of our nukes? They have plenty of their own. A lot of this isn't adding up. The big question is why Chernekov would pull some wild shit like this."

"That's why I asked you to be my chief of staff, Dee. You ask the right questions."

⇥ ⇤

Rolly thinks I ask the right questions. Fair enough. But what the hell are the answers? If Russia, the world's only other super power besides the United States, hijacked the *Louisiana* and kidnapped Matt, what can we do about it, short of all-out war? Chernekov may be an old-school KGB kind of guy, but he's not insane.

Or is he?

CHAPTER 5

I t's been two days since the *Louisiana* was hijacked and I became a hostage. Tony Riordan, my Chief of Staff , is in the stateroom next to me. We have no restrictions on speaking to one another, but we're careful what we say. Both Tony and I have checked every square inch of our living quarters and we couldn't find any bugs. We both like to be overly cautious.

We've been gone for two days. I assume that Rolly Benton has been sworn in as president under the 25th Amendment by now. At least the country is in able hands. But my thoughts drifted away from Rolly Benton, and shifted toward Dee. She takes up all of my consciousness. I love her as much now as I did the day we met. When I close my eyes, I can imagine the scent of her skin and hair, her beautiful body, and her never-ending smile. She has a mouth like a cab driver in traffic, and I even miss that. Right now, as I'm sitting here, Dee must think that I'm dead, just like everybody else. Not to be able to reach out and tell her I'm okay is an empty emotion that I can't get in touch with. I've never felt this way, because I've never been a prisoner before. When you're President of the United States, you grow accustomed to shaping events. You ask a question, and it gets answered. You see something you don't like, you make a phone call and it gets taken care of. You have a lot of power, enormous power. But now I don't even have the ability to move about freely. I have no power at all. I'm a prisoner.

The sub seems to be moving slowly, although I have no way of knowing other than my own senses. My guess is that they're trying to keep the *Louisiana's* audible footprint as obscure as possible.

"Tony, I assume that Rolly Benton was sworn in as president within an hour of our having gone missing."

Tony Riordan is what any president could wish for in a chief of staff. He's smart as hell, and doesn't take crap from anybody. He's a 6'2" black guy with the shoulders of a linebacker. But he handles his job less through physical intimidation than persuasion and leadership. Tony served four terms in the House of Representatives as a Congressman from Indiana. When his predecessor passed away suddenly, the Speaker of the House named him Chairman of the House Armed Services Committee and he was approved by unanimous vote from both sides of the aisle. *The New York Times*, not usually a fan of mine, praised my pick of Tony as White House Chief of Staff as a "brilliant appointment."

"Yes, Mr. President, I'm sure of it. The 25th Amendment is pretty strict about the office of the president not going vacant. They all assume that you're dead, I'm dead, and that the *Louisiana* has been destroyed. But Rolly Benton is a good man, sir. He won't consider this a closed case until he's convinced that there's no other explanation. He'll keep the seat warm for you, and FLOTUS, your beautiful wife, will keep the president on the scent of the hijackers. As you well know, sir, Dee Blake is one tough cookie. She won't fall for a bullshit plot like this."

⇥⊹ ⊹⇤

"Any guess where we're headed, Tony?"

"My guess is the Kola Peninsula, sir, the big Russian naval base, although now it's mainly a graveyard of broken down subs. Your thoughts, Mr. President?"

"I think we're heading to Balaklava on the Crimean Peninsula," I said. "Until 1996 it was the site of a huge underground submarine base. Now it's a museum. I've gotten intelligence briefings that Putin had plans to reopen it, and I'm sure that Boris Chernekov definitely intends to do so. If you want to hide an Ohio Class submarine, what could be better than an underground base? But the reality is we just don't know and we won't until we get there. It's hard to believe that the *Louisiana* is under the command of an American naval officer. Joe Campbell, from what I know about him, is a by-the-rules career officer. But if that's so, how the fuck can we believe that he's a head mutineer? The son of a bitch stole an American submarine, a submarine under his command, and kidnapped his president."

"I reviewed his service record, Mr. President, as soon as I learned about our visit to the *Louisiana*. There was no hint in the papers that he had a penchant for anything out of the ordinary. Just another mystery that we don't have answers for."

What Tony and I didn't know, but would find out after a Naval Board of Inquiry convenes, is that Campbell has been a member of the communist party all his adult life.

＝≑ ≑＝

"Good morning, gentlemen. I hope you enjoyed your breakfast," Admiral Yuschenko said, after knocking on our door and walking in.

"Good morning, Admiral," I said. "Thank you. Breakfast was fine, but I'm accustomed to choosing my own location and menu items. I have a question, well I have about a million questions, but for now can you tell us where we are? I don't see any security problem for you because we're obviously your prisoners. But it would be comforting to know where we are."

I'm not sure what "embarrassed" looks like, but that's exactly how Yuschenko's face appeared.

"Forgive me, Mr. President," Yuschenko said, "but I'm a military man. I follow orders, and my orders are not to disclose our location."

"Do you have any idea how long to our destination?" I asked.

"A matter of days, Mr. President. How many days I cannot say. Please relax and enjoy the comforts we give you. I have American movies on DVD discs that you can watch on the television. Please let me know if there is anything else you need."

Our friendly captor took his leave.

"What's your take on the admiral, Tony?"

"He strikes me as a guy who's following orders, Mr. President. I'm quite familiar with Russian military officers. They're tough and relentless about getting a job done. But there's something about Yuschenko that tells me he's going through the motions. Yeah, he's following orders, but I don't think he likes his orders."

"I get the same impression, Tony. Let's keep observing this guy—as best we can."

CHAPTER 6

We heard loud sounds on deck, which was surprising be-cause we were still submerged. For two hours we heard nothing but a steady cacophony of bangs, scraping, and commotion. Most of the noise seemed to come from the area of the conning tower, which is now called the sail, about 150 feet aft of us. Every few minutes, the sub would shudder as if grabbed by a giant. The noise went on unabated.

"Tony, do you have any idea what that noise and shaking is all about?"

"No, sir. I can't imagine what kind of work they could be doing while we're still under water."

When the noise finally stopped, the sub went silent for about an hour, except for short tapping sounds.

After 10 minutes, Tony and I both felt a change in the sea condition. The familiar thrum of the engines over the past few days was replaced by different sounds. We heard orders shouted and a lot of movement on deck. Tony, an Annapolis grad and former Navy man, has seen his share of sea duty.

"Those are the sounds of a special sea and anchor detail, Mr. President. We're tying up to a dock."

Admiral Yuschenko walked into our room. He wore a smile as usual. Something about This guy does not remind me of a kidnaper, I thought.

"You're being temporarily relocated, gentlemen. Please come with me. I think you will enjoy some fresh air."

We followed Yuschenko up the ladder onto deck. I wouldn't call the air fresh, but it was pleasantly different. What greeted us was an amazing site—a gigantic underground submarine base. I recognized it from photos as the sub base at Balaklava. Looks like my destination guess was accurate.

The space before us was breathtaking. I felt as if I was standing at the edge of an indoor football field looking across two others. A large doorway at one end suggested that more of the facility stretched beyond our vantage point. The walls appeared to be at least 100 feet high, topped by a curved ceiling, which was partially constructed of windows, giving the cavernous space an eerie glow of partial sunlight. I could see roller mechanisms and tracks across the ceiling and running down to the docks. My guess was that metal sheets could be rolled into place as a shield in case of a threatened attack. Along the bulkhead were docks for submarines. Across the walkway from each dock was a large door, apparently for on-loading supplies and large equipment. Only one other submarine occupied the gigantic space. It was tied up across from us about 300 feet away.

"Here's something that blows me away, Mr. President."

"What's that?" I asked.

"Do you realize that we entered this cave without surfacing?" Tony said. "From what I remember when I studied it, the sub base is carved into a huge cliff surrounding Balaklava Harbor. When it was fully operational they could dock as many as seven submarines at one time. Because a sub could enter or exit under water, they didn't have to worry about spy satellites seeing the boats come and go. More than 300 feet of rock sits atop 15 feet of reinforced concrete, creating a bomb shelter that could hold more than 3,000 people for 30 days. It gives me the creeps to think that Chernekov is dusting off this place to make it useable again as an active sub base."

"So, assuming that we keep this place under satellite surveillance, the *Louisiana* could come and go without our satellites noticing?" I said.

"That's right, Mr. President. Our arrival at Balaklava does nothing to change the story that we were hijacked. All that noise we heard as we approached was probably some external alterations to handle the tight squeeze through the tunnel. You've got to give these guys credit for one thing: they do a good job of preparation."

Our guards escorted us off the sub onto the dock. I could understand why sailors always talk about the first rubbery-leg feeling of stepping on dry land after a long cruise. Nausea swept over me. A chilly wind wafted through the facility, which I found pleasant. We walked for about a quarter of a mile and were taken to a wing of the base that appeared to be used for residential purposes. A sailor showed us into a suite with adjoining rooms and a common area in the middle. We checked for bugs as soon as we entered and found none.

Admiral Yuschenko knocked and walked in as we were having coffee in the common area.

"Gentlemen, I'm pleased to inform you that your submarine days are over, at least temporarily. You will be staying here until further notice."

"Admiral Yuschenko," I said, "What can you possibly have in mind? You have kidnapped the President of the United States and his Chief of Staff, as well as hijacked an American submarine. I don't see any possible scenario that turns out positive for you. Has

Boris Chernekov totally lost his grip on reality? Your country has committed an act of war and hopes to get away with it by subterfuge. This can't possibly work, and I think you know that. Using me or the *USS Louisiana* for negotiating purposes is idiotic. You may be able to pull this nonsense with a small powerless country, but not with the United States of America."

"Mr. President, with all due respect, sir, I am a military man simply doing my duty. Whether I believe these actions make sense is immaterial. Someone, presumably President Chernekov, has a plan, and I know nothing of the plan. I have recommended to you before and I say it again now, please think of yourselves as our guests and don't trouble yourselves with speculation."

"A guest, by definition, is free to leave when he wants to. So why don't you treat us as real guests and let us go?"

"That sounds like a simple solution, Mr. President, but life is not always so simple. I will be leaving you now. After my duties aboard the *Louisiana* are completed this afternoon, it's unlikely that you will see me again. It has been my pleasure to have met you."

I looked at Tony as the admiral walked out the door.

"That guy did not want this to happen and does not want it to continue." I said. "Something in my gut tells me that he's going to do something about it."

CHAPTER 7

"Please have a seat Admiral Yuschenko. Join me in some vodka?"
Yuschenko sat in the office of the new President of Russia,
Boris Chernekov. It was the same office that Vladimir Putin once
occupied. Chernekov, like his predecessor, preferred dark leather
and large spaces, adding to his feeling of power. Chernekov stood
at just under six feet. He had a barrel chest, partially from his former exercise routines and partially from genetics. His father was a
Russian general and also had a barrel chest, on which he sported
his medals, all of which he awarded himself. Chernekov, at 59 years
of age, was totally gray. His eyebrows were "bushy," and drooped
down over his eyeglasses.

"Thank you Mr. President, but it's a bit early in the day for vodka. I'll have some tea if you don't mind."

Chernekov snorted a laugh. "You call yourself a sailor? Suit yourself. So tell me Vasili, how is our guest, President Blake, faring?"

"Well, sir, as a prisoner he's faring about as well as can be expected. He speaks very little and when he does he asks questions,
as you would expect. We allow him to communicate with Tony
Riordan, his chief of staff. We see no risk, because they are sealed
off from the rest of the world."

"Vasili, we have big plans for Matthew Blake, not to mention the *USS Louisiana*."

"Sir, if I may," Admiral Yuschenko said, "what are our plans for President Blake and the *Louisiana*? I hope I'm not overstepping my bounds by asking."

"You *are* overstepping your bounds, Vasili. Your job is to follow and execute orders. Leave the speculation to us."

"Us?" thought Yuschenko, there is no "us." It's only him, Boris Chernekov. Yuschenko prided himself on his ability to conceal his contempt for Chernekov, a talent that helped keep him alive as a holdover from the prior administration. Yuschenko considered himself a patriot, and believed that Russia should be at the fore-front of world affairs, but not with the medieval skullduggery of Boris Chernekov.

"General Vladimir Zhukov will now take over the entertaining of our special guests," Chernekov said. "He will arrive at Balaklava this afternoon. Well done, Vasili. I commend you on how you carried out this assignment."

Zhukov? That's just great, thought Yuschenko. He's a sadistic brute if there ever was one, a perfect lackey to Chernekov, and now he's going to be in charge of guarding the President of the United States. When the word gets out, as it inevitably will, Russia will stand like swaggering whore before the world. This crazy operation gets stranger by the minute.

Yuschenko had an epiphany at the end of his meeting with Chernekov.

For the good of Mother Russia, I will personally put an end to this madness, he thought.

CHAPTER 8

I complain to myself about being too busy, but that's bullshit. The busier I am the less I think about Matt. The job of Chief of Staff to the President is an insane business, which is why the turnover is so high. During the Obama Administration, the average time on the job was one year—It's easy to see why. The job is like herding cats with a candle. The many tasks include daily administrative processes, paper flow, scheduling, and personnel decisions. On top of that, President Benton made it clear to me that my primary job is to solve the *Louisiana* mystery, the Matt Blake mystery. Of course that's why I took the position. Nobody in this country wants to see Matt Blake alive more than me. A thought that never leaves me, a thought that occupies every moment of my life, is that the most important person in my life is a prisoner—assuming he's alive.

I already received my on-the-job training during Matt's brief tenure in office by watching Tony Riordan do his work. Tony's a master of organization as well as diplomacy, a key requirement for the job of Chief of Staff. Because I was also a close advisor to Matt (more like the closest) I got to see Tony handle the office with grace and dedication. Matt told me—and he never bullshits with a subject like this—that he thought of me as a co-Chief of Staff. I hope I can do the same for Rolly Benton.

This afternoon I'll meet with people at the Office of Naval Operations. But this morning I had a major chore, one that required every bit of diplomatic skill I could muster. Both the senate majority leader and the speaker of the house are scheduled to meet with the President in the Oval Office. The subject is the new armed forces appropriations bill. This bill is a major item on the congressional agenda as well as the president's. One of Matt's campaign platforms was to strengthen the military, and President Benton is dedicated to seeing it through. A missing nuclear submarine provides a dramatic background to the meeting.

That the *Louisiana* may have been hijacked is now common thinking throughout the government. It's no secret, and the news media has picked up on it as well. That means that whoever stole the sub (presumably Russia) is aware of our knowledge. That means getting the appropriations bill through Congress fast, and putting in place whatever military contingencies we may face. The public awareness of our missing president and sub provides President Benton with a powerful bully pulpit. It's difficult for a member of congress to vote against a military appropriations bill in face of the action taken against the country. Of course, the various members saw the bill as an opportunity to slip in some vote-getting pork. A highway ramp leading to a constituent's new amusement park is just what the country needs. Matt and Rolly have more patience for this shit than I do.

I thought the meeting was a success, and I was happy with the way I handled it. You can't just stand up and say to two powerful members of congress that the president has a lot on his plate besides the appropriations bill, and that they need to move their asses. I managed not to piss them off, which I consider a win.

Last night I slept in my new quarters at Blair House, the president's guest facility across from the White House. Under the weird circumstances of the *Louisiana* disappearance, there were few guidelines for what to do with a First Lady who *may be* a former First Lady. My job as Chief of Staff makes it even more complicated. Not my problem. The government has protocol mavens who spend their time dwelling on bullshit questions like this.

Shortly after noon, I met with Admiral Spratt at the Office of Naval Operations.

"We have something, ma'am. I'm not sure what it is but here's what we know. Yesterday afternoon one of our listening devices picked up a submarine near the Crimean Peninsula. It's possible that it could be an Ohio Class, according to our experts, but we're not certain. This is meager evidence, but I wanted to let you know anyway."

"Do we know where the sub was headed?" I asked.

"We're almost certain it went to Balaklava, the former underground submarine base that's being reinstated. If you want to keep a submarine hidden, an underground facility is perfect."

"We need to keep satellite reconnaissance focused on that area," I said. "When the sub surfaces to enter the base, we'll have proof, proof for President Benton and for the United Nations if need be."

"Bad news, ma'am," the admiral said. "Balaclava is not just an underground facility, but it has an underwater entrance. A sub can enter and exit without surfacing. Our satellites will pick up nothing, I'm afraid."

I should have known that. When I did my study of submarines for Matt, I included the Russian submarine fleet. I completely missed the fact that Balaclava can be accessed without surfacing. But it was an unused museum at the time, and we had no intelligence that it was going to be returned to active service. I've got to stop beating myself over the head.

⇥⊦ ⊦⇤

"Good morning, this is Laura Ingraham calling for the First Lady, I mean the chief of staff, hell, you know who I mean."

"Laura, good to hear your voice, my friend," I said.

"Dee, honey, I can only imagine what you're going through. You and Matt had a marriage that I personally found inspirational."

"Make that present tense, Laura. Matt and I *have* a marriage."

"Of course, sorry Dee. Which kind of brings me to the point. I'm sitting in for Bill O'Reilly next Tuesday on the *O'Reilly Factor*, and I'd love to have you on the show. It's an open secret that the government believes that the *USS Louisiana* may have been hijacked, and that the president may be alive. You and I have been friends for a long time, Dee. You know that you don't have to worry about me asking questions that are too sensitive."

"And you know that I won't answer them," I said laughing. "I look forward to the show."

Perfect, I thought. Laura Ingraham has a huge audience. She knows how to ask tough questions, and I know how to answer them. One thing I've noticed about Laura over the years is that she never lets her journalistic duties interfere with her patriotism, and that's the kind of interviewer the country needs right now.

CHAPTER 9

Petty Officer James Tubin knocked on our door.

"General Vladimir Zhukov is here to see you, sir."

I couldn't believe the treasonous bastard called me "sir." I wondered how deep his involvement in the mutiny was. He must have been in pretty deep because he's still alive. The number of American defectors on this sub is one of the many ongoing mysteries of this surreal event.

A stockily built man, maybe 5'10", with broad shoulders, walked into our room. He wore the uniform of a Russian general with a chest full of medals. Not just service bars, but full medals that jingled when he walked. I guess he wanted to impress us with his military prowess. I just thought he was an asshole.

"Good morning, gentlemen, I am General Vladimir Zhukov of the Russian Army. I have been assigned to be your personal contact. You will notice that Admiral Yuschenko and I are of different personalities, and also of different beliefs when it comes to dealing with prisoners. He considered you our honored guests. I consider you our prisoners, and you will be treated accordingly."

Like Yuschenko, Zhukov spoke perfect English. Unlike Yuschenko, this prick had an attitude from hell.

"If I may offer an observation, General," I said, "we are not only your prisoners, we are your hostages. We've been kidnapped against all rules of international law and are being held against our will. This submarine, the *USS Louisiana,* is the property of the United States of America. You have committed an act of war, and you know it. Although I'm President of the United States, there is little I can do about your actions under the circumstances. I just hope that your new president knows what he's doing, because he isn't showing any evidence of it. The only positive outcome from this scenario is that you immediately return the *Louisiana* to the American government, along with the two of us and any other personnel that you're holding as prisoners. The longer this insane plan goes on, the worse will be Russia's position in the world."

Zhukov sat at the table, his medals rattling as he did. I think the schmuck sat down with a thud to make his medals jangle. He didn't ask to be seated, he just sat, and let out a hearty laugh, not of mirth but of sarcasm.

"I would expect that a man who has achieved such a high position as President of the United States would be more of a realist. Yes, you are our hostages as well as our prisoners. You may be thinking, given your typical American arrogance, that President Chernekov does not have an exact plan in mind. He does, and you fit into it. I realize that you can see no successful outcome for Russia, but you are wrong. We will succeed, you are our prisoners, escape is impossible, and that is all you need to know for now. I am removing the disc of American movies that Admiral Yuschenko supplied you. I believe your time is better spent reflecting on your situation. Good day, gentlemen."

CHAPTER 10

Thank God the job of White House chief of staff is so busy. It keeps my mind from wandering into dark places.

Matt and I have been married only six years, but it seems like we met yesterday. I was his client in a wrongful death lawsuit, which was the result of my husband Jim Spellman being killed in a car accident. Before I signed with Matt as an attorney, I went to one of his trials as an observer. Wow, he had me in the palm of his hands as he did the jury, and I think the judge. They awarded a multi-million dollar verdict—which, I later found out, was more than four times the amount of Matt's pre-trial demand. I was mesmerized by the way he communicated with the jury. He's tall, crazy handsome, and has a deep dramatic voice. I signed the legal retainer agreement right after that trial. No surprise, Matt achieved a gigantic settlement in my lawsuit. But the case was weird, not a simple sideswipe collision as we originally thought. Matt and his team discovered that Jim's accident may not have been caused by negligence, a typical personal injury or wrongful death case, but may have been murder. The evidence led to a huge conspiracy that reached the highest levels of government. My late husband,

Jim, was an investigative journalist. He was working on a series of articles on domestic terrorism that pointed in some embarrassing directions. I was Jim's editor and knew everything about his files as well as he did. Somebody wanted Jim dead, and me as well. The case became known as the *Sideswipe Conspiracy*. As a result of all this, Matt and I wound up in the FBI Witness Protection Program, the purpose of which was to keep us from getting our brains blown out. It wasn't an unpleasant experience by any stretch—Matt and I got married on our third day in the program at our secret undisclosed location in Lower Manhattan. You can't make this shit up.

After the criminal terror case closed, Matt and I moved back home to Chicago. The Windy City was, and still is, a crime infested place with horrible winters. But it was our home so we were happy to return, especially since we were no longer murder targets. I resumed my job as a professor of political science at Northwestern University, and Matt threw himself into the thriving negligence practice of Blake and Randolph. We kept growing closer, enjoying each other's company as much as we enjoyed our jobs. I think of Matt not only as my lover and husband, but as my best friend. When we have some time on our hands, we play catch. That's right, catch, with a ball and glove. At the White House we'd play catch in the hallway outside the Oval Office. It's a great highlight to our relationship. Try it.

As time went by I started to notice something about Matt. I began to realize that he wasn't just a great guy, with his good looks and sense of humor. It gradually dawned on me that I had married a great man. On the recommendation of a few people in government who knew him, Matt was appointed Deputy Secretary of Homeland Security. After only a few months on the job, he made a speech before congress to fill in for his suddenly ill superior. Matt was well known in Chicago for his prowess in front of jury. *The Chicago Tribune* once called him a "lion of the courtroom." The speech before Congress put him on the national map. Anyone who saw his speech on TV, as well as most network anchor people, asked the same question: "Who *is* this guy?"

I'll never forget the day that I suggested he run for President of the United States. We had both gotten home at the same time and sat down to chat over coffee. At first he thought I was kidding. He kept saying, "Me?" Then I explained to him that he was a war hero, with a chest full of decorations as a Marine captain. I also pointed out that he was a famous trial lawyer, and made a reputation as a magical communicator with his speech before Congress. He resisted—a lot. He pointed out that he had a checkered past as a heroin addict and alcoholic. But I told him that because he successfully shook the habits, it made him a heroic figure. I'm a former drunk druggie myself, so my words rang true with Matt. We both agreed that our ongoing battles with our mutual demons helped make us stronger—and closer. I think I clinched the decision when I told him that he's the kind of man that children should read about in history books.

So Matt tossed his hat in the ring, and ran for president against an egomaniacal scumbag named Bartholomew Martin, who ran on a ticket of preventing terror. Problem was, the campaign platform was bullshit because Martin and his group of thugs were terrorists themselves. Two weeks before the election a mysterious group (a group that everybody later suspected were Martin's henchmen) blew up a bunch of children's amusement parks, along with hundreds of children. The Martin campaign followed up with non-stop TV commercials warning of the dangers of terrorism. I remember the ads to this day: "Are you safe? Are your children safe? Our country needs Bartholomew Martin." The national panic swayed the vote in Martin's anti-terror direction. Matt lost.

The Martin administration became what people feared it would be, the beginning of the first American dictatorship. Every day another liberty disappeared. Matt and I saw our assets placed under seizure—for no stated reason. Our guns (which were totally legal) were confiscated, and our apartment was bugged. We feared the weekly "knock on the door." It seemed like we lived in a different country, one that became different overnight.

We weren't the only ones afraid of the loss of American liberty. A large group of people, myself included, convinced Matt to give the White House another shot in the next election cycle. With Matt's engaging oratory and tireless campaigning, the country looked to him as the man to save us from a totalitarian prick. I was with him every step of the way, flying around the country making endless campaign stops. It was tiring but fun at the same time. So Matt gave the presidency another shot—and won in a landslide.

The election was six months ago and Matt has been in office for four months. In his brief time as president he drastically changed the policies of Bartholomew Martin, the budding dictator, and almost single handedly returned America to the country we love.

Then Matt was kidnapped, and here I am. FLOTUS without a POTUS.

CHAPTER 11

P resident Boris Chernekov sat at the head of the table. He had convened a "meeting of ministers," which meant that he assembled a few people from whom he wanted information. Five men sat around the table facing the president, the Ministers of Commerce, Agriculture, Defense, Economy, and Education. Chernekov sat, cracking walnuts into a bowl and popping them into his mouth. He didn't offer any to the others.

"Mr. President," said Sergei Yakov, Minister of Commerce, "can you give us any details on the abduction of the American submarine and the President of the United States? We have been hearing constant rumors about this event."

"My dear Sergei," Chernekov said, his eyes squinting under his bushy eyebrows. "Why do you want to tie up valuable meeting time with talk of rumors? Are there not more important matters to discuss?"

"I'm sorry, sir, but I hear constant chatter about this event," Yakov said. "Perhaps, as your ministers, if we had more information we could help to handle the matter. I believe the Americans call it 'spin control.' It would seem that the hijacking of an American nuclear submarine, not to mention the kidnapping of the American

President, are all-pervasive issues, and the majority of Western press outlets thinks that Russia is complicit. I'm concerned about commercial relations between Russia and America. When I first heard of the event, I thought it must be fantasy. Never would we carry out such actions, I thought."

The other ministers present stared at the table in front of them. One fumbled through a file. Another checked his email. After Yakov stopped speaking, the room was silent. Chernekov, staring at Yakov, allowed the silence to linger. He put down his nut cracker and cracked his knuckles.

"Minister Yakov, perhaps you did not hear me correctly," Chernekov said. "There are some matters of which we speak, and others of which we remain silent. I don't know about these rumors you mention, and I have no comment on them. Does anyone else have something to say about the matter?"

No one spoke. Each man just shook his head.

Chernekov continued the meeting with reports about crop yields, armament procurement, a new school building program, and the status of the Russian and world economy. After he was done, Chernekov turned to Yakov.

"Minister Yakov, I notice that you don't have any reports on our commercial relations with other countries."

"Sir, ever since the rumors about the submarine and President Blake started," Yakov said, "nobody returns my calls. One person, from the Canadian Commerce Department, said that there could be no discussions of commerce until the mystery of the submarine and the American president is cleared up."

"Thank you, Sergei, for your persistent, if somewhat annoying, insistence on addressing your issue. Gentlemen, the meeting is over."

As the room emptied, Yakov turned to Chernekov and said, "Mr. President, may I have a word with you."

"Sergei, if your words aren't worth sharing with the others, they aren't worth sharing with me."

Yakov, who rated a car and driver because of his position as minister, climbed into the back seat of his renovated GAZ Chaika. He told the driver to take him to the eastern part of Moscow where he would attend a meeting with the Eurozone Manufacturing Consortium. Ten miles away from the Kremlin, where Yakov had just met with President Chernekov, the driver pulled into a vacant lot. The man got out of the car, opened the rear door, and fired three rounds into the head of Sergei Yakov from his Makarov pistol. Another car pulled alongside, and the driver of Yakov's vehicle climbed into the front passenger seat.

The world press reported that Yakov had been shot in a holdup.

CHAPTER 12

"Have a seat, Captain," I said. "How about a cup of coffee."

"Thank you, Mrs. Blake, I'd enjoy that. I'm not used to meetings starting at 7 a.m."

"Get used to it, Captain," I said. "Until we solve this crisis, think of 7 a.m. as noon."

I was sitting in my office with Captain Wallace Keaton, the head of the Office of Naval Intelligence (ONI). The United States boasts (boasts?) 17 separate intelligence agencies, ONI being one of them. Keaton has spent his entire career—18 years so far—with ONI. Pundits constantly shake their heads about the duplication of intelligence information in the US. Are there turf wars? Yes. Do agencies overstep their bounds? Yes. Does the right hand occasionally forget what the left hand's doing? Yes. But one good thing about all of these spies running around is that if the president wants an answer to a question, he just has to make a couple of phone calls. Personally, I have no problem with all the duplication. Better too much information than not enough.

"Captain," I said, "you're going to see a lot of me in the near future. Today, there's one major issue I want to discuss: Captain

Joseph Campbell, commanding officer of the *USS Louisiana*. He was in command when the sub went missing. What do we know about this guy?"

"His service record is clean as a whistle, ma'am. After he graduated from Annapolis, he was assigned to the nuclear power program. He rose through the ranks, having served on eight different submarines in his 18 year career to date. He's never had a negative comment in his service record."

"His service record?" I said, a bit too loudly. "You head up the Office of Naval Intelligence and all you can tell me is that his service record is clean? There are only two possibilities, Captain. Either Campbell's been killed or captured, or he's complicit in a mutiny. We need to know a lot more about this guy. Have you checked his financial records?"

"No, ma'am, but we probably should. It will take a while to get a warrant to check his financial accounts."

I picked up the phone and dialed the office of Sarah Watson, Director of the FBI. I put it on speaker so Captain Keaton could hear.

"This is Chief of Staff Blake. Please put me through to the director."

Sarah Watson was in a meeting, but interrupted it to take my call.

"Sarah, I need a warrant, ASAP. We need to check the financial records of Captain Joseph Campbell, the CO of the *Louisiana*. We need it NOW, and I need to cut short the process."

"We're ahead of you, Dee. I got the warrant two days ago and we're checking his records as we speak."

Watson's assistant waved his hands to get her attention, and pointed to a folder he had just placed on her desk.

"I just received an update, Dee, and it's in front of me right now."

"Please check it while we're on the phone, Sarah."

I realized that I was being a total pain in the ass, making demands that Sarah Watson seldom hears. But she's used to dealing with the White House. Now she'll have to get used to me.

"Holy shit," said Watson. "I'm reading the briefing now. Last month the tidy sum of 10 million dollars was deposited into one of Campbell's accounts—an American bank account. The Navy must have raised its pay rates."

"Have you been able to track the source of the funds, Sarah?"

"Not yet, Dee. I don't expect to find a hot trail. Whoever paid him this money was clumsy enough to deposit the funds in a domestic bank account, and I doubt that they'd be so stupid as to leave fingerprints on the source. We're also checking the financial records of every sailor and officer on the *Louisiana*."

After I got off the phone with Sarah Watson, I looked at Captain Keaton, the ONI honcho, who appeared chastened. Is this asshole in charge of Naval Intelligence or Naval Stupidity? I wondered.

"Captain, please coordinate your efforts with the FBI," I said. "They're on top of this case."

"Yes, ma'am," Keaton said. "ONI sometimes doesn't move as fast as it should."

I just stared at him.

⊷⊷

I met with President Benson for our regularly scheduled morning briefing.

"We're seeing the early indications of a high level mutiny, Mr. President" I said. "The sub captain's assets swelled by 10 million last month. The money was deposited in an American bank account if you can believe that. The FBI is doing similar checks on every crew member."

"We've been assuming it was the Russians," President Benton said. "Do you think this could be a simple mutiny? If so, what do they expect to get from it? So somebody put the 10 million into the captain's account. It looks like this may be a combination of a mutiny and a foreign hijacking. But the question still remains—why? I think it's time for me to call Boris Chernekov, the new Russian President. He called me the day of the *Louisiana* event to give me condolences and bullshit offers of assistance. Everything in my gut tells me the Russians are involved. If it *was* a mutiny, that doesn't mean there wasn't outside help."

CHAPTER 13

"Tony, have you noticed the accents on the sailors in the hallways?"

"Yes, Mr. President. Mainly American accents and only occasional Russian. I think this was a Russian hijacking combined with an American mutiny. Every intelligence agency is on top of this, I'm sure. Let's face it; we're in the dark. And even if we knew the answers, we don't know the answer to the big question—what the hell are they up to?"

<hr>

General Zhukov, our new host, walked into the room. He didn't knock, didn't clear his throat, he just walked in, the medals on his chest jingling. It probably wouldn't help the situation if I punched this guy's lights out, but that's exactly what I felt like doing.

"Mr. President," he said. "Your living arrangements will be going through a few changes. You and Mr. Riordan will no longer be in adjacent rooms but will occupy separate quarters."

"But what could the problem be with Mr. Riordon and me in the same suite? We're cut off from the world, obviously. Why can't we be together?"

"My orders are not to answer questions. My orders are to give orders. You will now come with me and my comrades."

We were placed in blindfolds—fucking blindfolds. My handler escorted me down a long corridor where I was shoved, not too gently, into a room. It wasn't the pleasant quarters we had gotten used to; it was more like a prison cell. There was a short cot, barely able to contain my 6'3" body. The room was 10 by 9 feet. A toilet adorned the corner of the room, along with a sink. There was a small shower stall that gushed water with the enthusiasm of a leaky pipe. The water was cold. Just as well—there was no soap. No windows, no mirrors, just a blank cell, with an ashtray full of stubbed-out cigar butts. I asked if I could have some reading material, but my handler simply slammed the door shut. Time to think. I had nothing else to do, so I figured I may as well. In the Marines, I'd been involved in enough interrogations to recognize that they were playing with our heads. Solitary confinement is a powerful psychological weapon. With nobody to talk to, your mind wanders from one thought to the next. But why the hell are they doing this? As President of the United States, I'm privy to a lot of top secret information. Maybe that's what they're after. I had no idea. Maybe they're just trying to grind me down mentally so I can't give a clear explanation of this crap if we ever get out of here.

They also took my watch, so I had no way to tell time. My prison cell was located on an interior corridor, so I couldn't even count the days by sunrise and sunset. I was in total sensory deprivation.

It doesn't matter what kind of training you've had, and I had the best with the Marines. Yes, we did go through solitary confinement scenarios, but they didn't last long, and they were tempered by the knowledge that it was just a training exercise. I realized that it doesn't matter what position you hold. Forget that I'm the President of the United States. The simple fact is that I'm a prisoner in solitary confinement.

I asked for writing materials so I could jot notes for myself. Don't know why I bothered. Nothing happened. Solitary, according to these guys, is solitary, and that means no reading, no writing. Just be there. I've studied the effects of solitary confinement on prisoners, and it's definitely an extreme type of detention, bordering on torture. A lack of human interaction becomes painful after a while. Your mind feeds on memories, both good and bad.

I tried to organize my time, whatever the hell time it was, by exercising, something I love to do. 20 pushups, followed by 20 sit ups, followed by a bunch of different leg and arm stretching exercises. That took up 30 minutes, which left me with 23 hours and 30 minutes to account for.

I thought about Dee. She's not just my wife, but the love of my life, my best friend. She's sure that I'm dead, I thought. Everybody thinks I'm dead. Not being able to reach out to her to say I'm okay was the worst part of my confinement. Dee is 39 years old and beautiful. If there is such a thing as objective beauty, Dee's it. Her hair, her eyes, her gorgeous body—hey stop. What the hell am I doing, I thought, besides torturing myself? I should be able to come up with a match for her. Maybe Rolly Benton. He's a good-looking guy, a solid citizen, and he comes from an excellent background. He's President of the United States, no less. Problem is, Rolly is almost 20 years older than Dee. When she's 65 he'll be 85. No, gotta be somebody younger.

Now what the fuck am I doing? I'm flagellating myself with thoughts about finding a suitable mate for *my* mate. I'm not used to being dead, not in the eyes of other people. But dead I am, and so is Tony. We disappeared in a submarine followed by an explosion.

I don't know all the evidence, but I'm sure these bastards made it look convincing.

Evidence? If there's one thing I've convinced Dee about, it's to distrust evidence. When she helped me prepare for trial, I could see that she internalized my warning—don't trust the evidence. Finally, I came up with a positive thought. Our government may have information that I don't know about. When the incident occurred, all I felt was the sudden gyration of the sub, followed by the explosion. Admiral Yuschenko seemed to think it was a flawless operation, but what would you expect the guy in charge to say? There may be evidence that I don't know about, evidence that may convince Dee that I'm alive.

I need a way to tell time, if only to keep my head from exploding.

As a kid I once memorized the Gettysburg Address for a school assembly. The speech was 272 words and took three minutes to recite. If I recited it five times in a row it would take 15 minutes. After that I would meditate for 20 minutes. I have long practiced meditation, so I knew internally when 20 minutes went by. After meditation, I would recite the Gettysburg Address another five times. Next came my exercise routine, which I knew was exactly 30 minutes. Then I factored in 20 minutes of free-form thinking. This process—the recitation, the meditation, exercise, and free-form thinking—all took up an hour and a quarter. I found a can opener lying in a corner of my room. I used it to cut notches into the floor, each notch representing an hour. The last time I looked at my watch was before I was transferred to my new quarters. I thought it was 0900—three hours ago, by my estimate. So that's my starting point – 12:00, Thursday, October 1. At least I had a method of measuring time. Not precise, but close enough for prisoner work.

Okay, time to get to work:

"Four score and seven years ago our fathers brought forth on this continent a new nation, conceived in liberty, and dedicated to the proposition that all men are created equal.

Now we are engaged in a great civil war, testing whether that nation, or any nation so conceived and so dedicated, can long endure. We are met on a great battlefield of that war. We have come to dedicate a portion of that field, as a final resting place for those who here gave their lives that that nation might live. It is altogether fitting and proper that we should do this.

But, in a larger sense, we cannot dedicate, we cannot consecrate, we cannot hallow this ground. The brave men, living and dead, who struggled here, have consecrated it, far above our poor power to add or detract. The world will little note, nor long remember what we say here, but it can never forget what they did here. It is for us the living, rather, to be dedicated here to the unfinished work which they who fought here have thus far so nobly advanced. It is rather for us to be here dedicated to the great task remaining before us—that from these honored dead we take increased devotion to that cause for which they gave the last full measure of devotion—that we here highly resolve that these dead shall not have died in vain—that this nation, under God, shall have a new birth of freedom—and that government of the people, by the people, for the people, shall not perish from the earth."

During the free-thinking part of my time-keeping routine, I wondered how long it would take to carve those words into General Zhukov's skull with my can opener. Solitary confinement can make for nasty thoughts.

CHAPTER 14

Matt thinks that we believe he's dead. I can't get that thought out of my mind. Our theory, and I think it's solid, is that the loss of the *Louisiana* was faked, along with the debris-laden explosion. Does Matt know that? I doubt it. All he probably knows was that the *Louisiana* was hijacked and an explosion was set off to cover it. He's a prisoner, God knows where, and he thinks that the world has bought the story, which means that he thinks that *I* think he's dead. This is the creepiest thought I can imagine. I love Matt as much as my own life, and there's nothing I can do to reach out to let him know we're on top of the situation, that I'm waiting for him. But I'm a widow as far as he knows.

Matt had a good working relationship with now President Rolly Benton. They were also good friends. Matt's probably thinking that Rolly has politely cut me off from the White House, and that I'm starting a new life as the former First lady, a new life as a widow. I think he'd be shocked to know that President Rolly has made me his Chief of Staff. That's because Matt doesn't know what we know.

It isn't easy being a widow to a man you deeply love. It's even worse being a widow when you're not.

I looked at my watch. It was 7:15 a.m., well into the daily schedule of the workaholic Rolly Benton.

"Mr. President," I said, "the Prime Minister of India is due in a half-hour. We should go over your briefing papers."

India was a good ally of the United States, but, like most allies, not one without difficulties. Prime Minister Narendra Modi was a good man, but a well-known ball buster on matters of trade. Especially since the disappearance of the *Louisiana*, President Benton knew it was time to shore up any cracks in relations with the country's allies. He shocked Prime Minister Modi with his offer of most favored nation (MFN) status as a trading partner. Of course he didn't bring this up early in the conversation, but saved it for the end, a good way to send the man away happy.

⊨≍⊨ ≍⊨

After the Prime Minister left, Rolly asked me to stay for a brief meeting.

"Dee, Admiral Spratt, the submarine boss, apparently has some new information for us. I just got a call from CNO Ashley Patterson. See him as soon as you can, and let me know the outcome."

New information? I thought. If it's new, why the hell didn't they bring it to my attention before?

CHAPTER 15

"Admiral Spratt is here to see you, Mrs. Blake," the receptionist said. "Admiral Patterson is with him."

Ashley Patterson—Chief of Naval Operations. Spratt's bringing the boss. They must have something important to talk about.

"Good morning, Admiral Spratt," I said. "Hi, Ashley. So you folks have something new about the *Louisiana*?"

"A few things, Mrs. Blake," Admiral Spratt said. "The first concerns personnel and the follow-up to the ONI and FBI investigations. Of the 15 officers and 140 enlisted personnel, we have found financial irregularities in the records of fully half of them. That's seven officers and 70 sailors. Nothing as dramatic as the $10 million that showed up in Captain Campbell's account, but enough to make us want to continue investigating."

"Also, we've tested each piece of debris found in the ocean near the site in question," Spratt said. "Apparently somebody didn't get the memo. New naval procurement standards require that a bar code be inscribed on each piece of equipment designated for every ship, sub, plane, or vehicle in the Navy. Not one piece of debris from the *Louisiana* incident had any bar code—not one. Simply stated, to emphasize what you noticed immediately, the debris did not come from the *Louisiana*. As you put it, Mrs. Blake, the debris field was a bullshit yard sale."

I let that news wash over me like a warm bath. Further evidence that Matt's alive.

"But the big thing we want to talk to you about are the nuclear missiles on the *Louisiana*," Ashley Patterson said. "We're concerned—I'm concerned—that they can be retargeted."

"But doesn't the procedure call for a launch code from the President himself?" I asked. "The codes are updated daily, and I personally supervise that operation as I did this morning. How can the missiles possibly be activated?"

"The current launch code procedure is one that we've designed for our own purposes and security," Ashley said. "Nothing technical requires the launch code procedure, especially with the boat in enemy hands. It would take some serious engineering knowledge, but the missile battery can be reconfigured to a launch-on-command method. What I'm saying, Dee, is that the *Louisiana* can be turned into a lone wolf stalking the oceans."

"All of which brings us back to the central question," I said. "Why? The Russians have enough of their own nukes to destroy us and we have enough to destroy them. Why the hell would they go through an elaborate deception to steal one of our subs? Of course they'll get useful intelligence as they pick the bones of our submarine technology. But why? Can anybody give me an answer to that?"

"You're talking about strategic matters that are over my paygrade, Dee," Admiral Patterson said, "but the simple answer to your question is that I don't know. If it *is* the Russians, it doesn't seem to make any sense. Do you really think that Boris Chernekov is willing to make a horse's ass out of himself by trying to trade our president and a nuclear submarine for a deal of some sort? Russia would be made to stand in a corner wearing a dunce cap at the UN

General Assembly. The facts—as we think we know them—simply don't add up."

"Maybe it isn't the Russians," Admiral Spratt said.

Ashley and I looked at him.

"What's your thinking, Pete?" Ashley asked.

"We *think* it was the Russians, because they're the only ones sophisticated enough to pull something like this off. If it *was* them, can we be sure the Russians will control matters going forward? In other words, is it the Russians who hope to benefit from this plot, or is some other player involved?"

"When President Benton spoke to Chernekov the other day, he was positive that the Russians had pulled it off," I said. "But if I understand you, the Russians may have done the deed and will now pass it off to another country?"

"Yes, ma'am, that's exactly what I'm saying," Admiral Spratt said.

"But what country?" I said. "China? They're in the same position as the Russians. They have their own arsenal. If they wanted to make war, all they need to do is decide. The Islamic State? A ridiculous idea. They know how to make IEDs and suicide bomb vests. Handling a nuclear submarine is a couple of hundred years beyond them."

"What about Iran?" Ashley said. "Remember, they have a new regime, a radical new regime. The current ayatollah makes the rantings of Ahmadinejad sound like Sunday school lectures. Abad Tavana, the new ayatollah, is, for lack of a better description, a messianic nut case. I could easily picture him as a pal of Chernekov. More than any other mullah we've dealt with, that man is committed to the idea that the Twelfth Imam will appear and the infidels will die in a conflagration."

"I have a lot to brief the president on," I said. "Anything else you can think of?"

"Just one thing," said Spratt. "Our deep-dive subs and sonar arrays haven't picked up anything that could be the wreckage of a submarine. Further evidence for your theory."

"And further evidence that Matt's alive," I said.

━━┤+┝━━

I met with the president and briefed him on my latest meeting with Naval Operations. Every time I enter the Oval Office, which is quite often, I'm hit in the face by a stark reality. Just a few days ago, this was my husband's office. I can see Matt sitting behind the desk. I can hear his voice, smell his cologne. I think Rolly is aware if that, which is why we often meet in another room.

"Mr. President, according to the head of NavOps our problem could be getting worse," I said. "Admiral Patterson explained to me in detail how the sub's missile firing capabilities can be changed. After a few modifications, a presidential authentication won't be necessary for a launch. She also described how the targets for the missiles can be reconfigured. Bottom line, sir, the *Louisiana* can be used against us. We can only speculate on what their plans are for my husband."

"And we're still left to ponder the biggest question of all—why?" the President said.

CHAPTER 16

I found it disconcerting that the president relied so much on me and my memory of events and conversations. I guess I should feel flattered, but it gives me a ton of anxiety to be entrusted with so much power.

"Dee, I want you to meet with CIA Director Carlini. He has people inside places that we could only guess. Because those spies live in the shadows, they can see things hiding in shadows. That's why we call them spooks. Bill Carlini and his people are key to unraveling this mess.

⊷⊶

William Carlini had been CIA Director for 10 years, minus four years when he was replaced in the administration of Bartholomew Martin. Matt told me that picking Bill Carlini to head the CIA was an easy choice. Carlini is well known, not only throughout the government, but across the world as a smart, gutsy guy who doesn't trust anything until he sees proof. I've met him a couple of times before, and I'm convinced that he's the real deal.

A CIA police officer from the Security Protective Service met me and my secret service agents at the entrance to CIA headquarters in Langley, Virginia. The CIA has its own cops, no surprise. We were escorted to Carlini's office, and my secret service guys waited outside the door. The office was spacious, about 20 by 30 feet, enabling him to call a sudden large meeting. I found it annoyingly dark. The walls were deep walnut, the carpet rich brown, and all of the furniture either black or dark brown. I asked him why all the darkness.

"Spooks like to lurk in the shadows," he said.

I noticed immediately that he wasn't alone.

"I believe you recognize your old friend, Buster," Carlini said. He was referring to Agent Gamal Akhbar, the best spy in the CIA, and a good friend. Buster, as everybody calls him, is a tall Middle Eastern-looking guy. He gets his looks from his Lebanese mother. He's a Christian, speaks fluent Arabic, and often refers to himself as a jihadi's worst nightmare.

Buster stood and extended his hand. We're good enough friends that a brief hug would have been in order, but Buster is a stickler for appearances.

"Buster, as you know, is usually 10 steps ahead of the rest of us," Carlini said. "I'm going to ask you, Madam First Lady, to bring us up to date on what you've heard from NavOps, and then Buster will fill us in on where we are."

"Bill," I said, "thank you for honoring me with my fancy title, but as we all know I'm the *former* First Lady—until further notice— and the current Chief of Staff to President Benton. I look forward to reclaiming my old title as First Lady, Matt's wife, but for now, please call me Dee."

I brought them up to date on the latest thinking at Naval Operations, including Admiral Patterson's concern about the launch codes and targeting procedures being reconfigured.

"So here is our current thinking," I said. "We have a suspicion that the *Louisiana* may be docked on the Crimean Peninsula at the old underground submarine base at Balaklava. We know that a submarine entered the facility a few days ago, but we're stumped about something. We picked up a faint return on sonar of a sub with characteristics like an Ohio, but that's the only thing we have to go on. We have the entrance and exit from Balaklava under tight satellite surveillance, but that doesn't do much for us because a sub can enter and exit the underground base while submerged."

"Has the Navy limited its surveillance to Russian facilities, Dee?" Buster asked.

"Yes," I said. "Our whole concept is that this was pulled off by the Russians. Who else would have the capability of executing such an event? But of course, that doesn't answer why Russia would do such a stupid thing—steal one of our subs and kidnap the president."

Nobody seems to have the answer to that question.

CHAPTER 17

Without my invented method of keeping time, I think I would have lost my mind by now. I had just finished my hour and a quarter routine. First the Gettysburg Address repeated five times, then meditation, then exercise, followed up by just plain thinking. I estimate that three days have gone by according to the can opener notches I made in the floor. A sound at my door told me that my food, if you can call it that, was about to be delivered. A sailor walked in, whom I recognized as an American from my initial introductions a few days ago. He put my tray down on a table next to my cot.

"Hey sailor," I said, "can you get me some cleaning supplies? Some spray disinfectant, a sponge, a mop, stuff like that."

"I'm sorry sir, but I'm not allowed to take any requests."

With that, he looked over his shoulder and set down a new toothbrush and a tube of toothpaste next to it. He smiled and nodded as he did that.

"Thank you," I said. "Anything going on?" I didn't really expect an answer, but I just welcomed the interaction with another human being, especially one bearing toothpaste.

"General Zhukov will be by this afternoon, sir."

The kid was polite, even though I was his prisoner, and even though the little prick was a traitor.

"Thank you Petty Officer—what's your name?"

"Jackson, sir, Phil Jackson."

"Well, thank you Petty Officer Jackson, a pleasure speaking to you."

"I'll try to sneak in some cleaning stuff, sir," he said softly.

It looked like I may have made a friend, if you can call a traitor a friend.

After I finished my meal of diced beets and mashed potatoes, I began my next recitation of the Gettysburg Address.

"Four score and seven years ago..."

CHAPTER 18

"Matt, wake up," I screamed as I shook him. He didn't move and I shook him again. But it wasn't him. It was a pillow. Matt wasn't there.

Nightmares were becoming a regular part of my life. Matt is the most important person in my world, and being without him gives me an unshakeable feeling of emptiness. Thank God President Benton has given me a busy job. Otherwise I think I'd lose my mind.

I looked at the time on the radio display. Shit, 3:30 a.m. and I was wide awake. God could I use a drink, I thought. A couple of vodkas would make things a lot more pleasant.

What the hell am I thinking? Absolutely not. Both Matt and I are former (that is, *recovering*) substance abusers. After my first husband died, I began to hit the bottle heavily, and then included drugs in my diet. I was a full spectrum substance abuser—booze, drugs, and food. In the space of a year and a half, I had ballooned into 250 pounds, a fat, drunk, self-indulgent slob.

Thank God a good friend intervened and got my ass into re-hab, the Monahan Institute in Milwaukee, Wisconsin, a great place run by a great man, Jake Monahan. I didn't know Matt at the time, but we later learned that we were both graduates of the Monahan Institute. With Monahan's help, I went on a regimen of diet, meditation, constant exercise, and therapy, slimming down to my current size, which Matt says is perfect. When I first met Matt, I have to admit that I looked pretty good. On our first date, we discovered that we were *both* alcoholic drug addicts. It was a turning point in our brief relationship. We spilled our guts to each other that night. I told Matt about waking up on the floor of a jail cell after I got drunk on a park bench the night before. He told me about getting a case dismissed because he nodded off on heroin and missed a court date. We realized that we had something more in common than a mutual attraction to each other. We fought the same demons. That night we were both exhausted. We expected an evening of passion, but we woke up in the morning sitting on the couch with my head on Matt's shoulder. It was perfect, not exciting, but perfect. Two days later, on a Monday, I showed up unannounced in Matt's office with a simple message:

"I love you."

He said the same. I realized that whatever life held for me, it would include Matt Blake. Our lives have been one ever since.

My imagination didn't include the idea that the man I married would become President of the United States, or that he would be kidnapped.

⊶ ⊷

My mind wandered to a wonderful morning just a few weeks ago. Matt and I lay in bed after awakening.

"Hey, Dee, is it me or was last night unbelievable?"

"No, Matt. Last night *was* believable. We both went through it, again, and again, and again. I believe it. Do you?"

"So what happened, Dee, besides the best night of sex we ever had? Did something change for the better?"

"Honey, when you ran for this job as President of the United States, we both knew it would be stressful as hell. We both knew it would mess with our private lives. But last night, after four months on the job, we've finally achieved a breakthrough. Last night we learned to box out your job, and to box in our relationship. Last night was just about us."

"Hey, what are you doing?" Matt asked.

"You have to ask?"

"The alarm is set for 5:30, Dee."

"Do you want me to stop?" I said, as I lifted my head and looked at him.

"I did *not* say that."

"We have 45 minutes," I said. "Plenty of time to sound a few more alarms. Now let me get back to what I was doing."

No way am I going to go back to my old ways. I came close to destroying my life once, and I'm done with that shit. But even more important, I felt that a drink would be a betrayal of Matt, and that's the last thing in the world I'd want to do.

Now I have to find Matt.

CHAPTER 19

Ali Behzadi sat in his office in Tehran with his old friend Basim Rouhani. Both men were in their mid-60s. Behzadi's office was equipped with modern functional furniture that was also quite comfortable, which he required because of arthritis in his lower back. The office overlooked a grove of fig trees, which Behzadi loved because the view took his mind off his constant back pain.

Both men were known as mullahs or religious leaders. They were revered by people because of their positions, their titles, and also because people were attracted by their peaceful manners.

"Basim, my friend, I think that you and I have strayed from the black and white message of our regime over the past few years. Let's face a simple fact. You and I really do see Islam as a religion of peace, but we are rare. Our people have had their heads pounded over the years with a message of hate. They forget that the Quran, as dictated to the Prophet, may peace be upon him, was written down by primitive semi-literate tribespeople. You and I are both familiar with the possible differing interpretations of the Quran. One passage is interpreted to say, 'Find the non-believer and smite him before the justice of Allah.' That very same passage has been interpreted by others as, 'Embrace the non-believer and show him the way to the love of Allah.' In other words, Basim, as you and I have discussed many times, the leadership of our nation has chosen to interpret the Quran as a message of fear and hatred."

"Are you talking about 'Death to America,' Ali?" Rouhani said with a laugh.

"Yes, Basim, that's a perfect example. You and I have both lived and studied in the United States when we attended NYU many years ago. I found America to be an open, free society, where all religions are welcome to worship in their own way. Can America be a bully at times? Of course. As the most powerful nation on earth, its leaders sometimes think that they can determine the future for other countries. A perfect example is when they supported that dictator Pahlavi as the Shah of Iran. But the sheer stupidity of capturing the American Embassy and holding 52 people hostage for over a year strains my imagination. 'Death to America' became part of the Iranian vocabulary, but it gradually came to hold as much meaning as 'good morning.' "

"You're correct, Ali. The leadership of our country embraced the idiots who took over the embassy, and even helped them. We forced a world crisis that had no meaning, other than to the religious fanatics who were in charge. We picked a fight with the most powerful nation on earth, and what did we have to show for it? Crippling economic sanctions and political turmoil. It was a sad time for Iran."

"Our country now has a new name for the United States," Ali said—"'the Great Satan.' Forgive me my friend, but I can say this to few people other than you. I find nothing 'satanic' about the Great Satan. Any rational political leader would see that friendship and cooperation with America is in our own self-interest. Can you imagine a better trading partner? But no, we now have a regime that is even worse than the ones in years past. We have a regime that wants to drill the idea of the Great Satan into our people's heads. As we well know, Basim, vast numbers of Iranians don't accept this idiocy. Sure, the regime can line up a few hundred young men screaming 'Death to America,' but you and I know, as do most people, that these are staged events for TV cameras. The average Iranian would just as soon see America as a partner. But that is less likely to happen now than it has been for decades. Abad Tavana, our new supreme leader, is a messianic cult believer. I think he is truly insane, but that doesn't matter. He has control over the people in government, and our relations with the United States will continue to deteriorate. No matter what problem Iran faces, including storms and earthquakes, Tavana has a simple answer— the Great Satan."

Rouhani leaned forward and lowered his voice, a habit he had learned over the years.

"Ali, do you think our regime has anything to do with the capture of that American submarine and the kidnapping of the President of the United States? I hear constant rumors, which is normal in our country. However, one of my sources of information I consider to be solid. My old friend Farhad Asidi has worked in the foreign ministry for many years. He is still there because he knows when to keep his mouth shut. Farhad tells me that he's sure it's the Russians who are behind the conspiracy. That much you and I could have guessed by ourselves. But Farhad thinks that there's another force behind the caper."

"But besides Russia, Basim, who could possibly be behind this crazy scheme?"

"I have no idea, but whoever it is must be intimately familiar with America and its ways."

CHAPTER 20

I had just completed the Gettysburg Address, part of my odd-ball way of keeping time, when everything went dark. My sole light bulb had blown out and I sat in total darkness. My routine, for what it was worth, was suddenly dashed into nothing. I couldn't even scratch hash marks into the floor because I couldn't see the floor. I hit the solid core of sensory deprivation.

Because of my time-keeping routine, I had an idea that my watcher, Petty Officer Jackson, would soon come to deliver my meal. I estimated that he would appear in about 10 minutes.

Didn't happen. Besides total darkness, I would go without my meal of soggy potatoes and raw beets. As much as I hated the fare, the thought of it was good because I was hungry as hell. I had actually cut down on my exercise program by a few minutes, because my protruding ribs told me that I wasn't getting enough calories. I was famished.

General Zhukov was obviously fucking with my head, and doing a good job of it. This guy must have been a big hit with the KGB. He's a sadistic prick who does things for no reason, other than because he can.

After what I estimated to be a couple of hours, I heard the door open. No knock, no warning, just an opening door. The faint ambient light from the hallway actually stung my eyes.

"Good afternoon, Mr. President," said Zhukov. "I trust that you have been able to relax without interference from a light bulb."

I squinted at him and noticed that he wasn't carrying a food tray.

I guessed that he expected that I'd beg, plead, and protest my lack of light and food. Instead, I just said "Good afternoon, General."

He reached overhead and unscrewed the dead light bulb, replacing it with a glaring beast that must have been over 1,000 watts. I felt like I was on an operating table without anesthesia.

He said nothing more. He just turned and left the room, leaving me to ponder my new suddenly bright surroundings and wondering when or if I'd ever eat again. The man was a talented brain fucker.

CHAPTER 21

"Director Carlini, a Mrs. Ludmila Yushcenko is here to see you sir," his assistant said. "She's accompanied by a lawyer. I don't have her down as an appointment."

"Find out exactly what they want and let me know," Carlini said. He had a firm rule not to entertain visitors unless they had an appointment with completely spelled-out business.

"She says that she wants to discuss immunity for herself and her husband," Johnston said.

"Direct them to the State Department. I don't discuss immunity matters."

"Sir, she says it concerns the *USS Louisiana.*"

Carlini sprang to his feet, spilling a glass of water all over the papers on his desk.

"Send them up immediately. Call Buster and tell him to come to my office."

Buster approached Carlini's door at the same time as Mrs. Yuschenko and her lawyer.

"Hi Buster, long time no see," said the lawyer.

"Jack Townsend, my friend and former CIA spook, and now criminal defense lawyer. You're looking well and prosperous. Come in. The director is waiting for us."

They walked into Carlini's spacious office. It was raining heavily and windswept drops pelted the windows. The overcast skies added to the darkness of the room, so Carlini turned on all the lights.

"Hello, Jack," Carlini said to Townsend. "I hope private practice is suiting you well. If you ever want to come back to the side of goodness and truth, we'd love to have you. My assistant says that you want to discuss the *USS Louisiana* as well as some sort of immunity deal. You realize that we're also talking about the status of the President of the United States."

"Yes, sir, I represent Ludmila Yuschenko and her husband Admiral Vasili Yuschenko. The admiral will be here in a couple of days for a naval conference at the Pentagon, and Ludmila said that she's here to pave the way for him. Because of the sensitive nature of what we'll be discussing, I'm asking for immunity from prosecution for Ludmila. Then we'll discuss Admiral Yuschenko."

"Granted, Jack. Just hand me the piece of paper. You're lucky I know you, otherwise I wouldn't short circuit the process."

"Ludmila speaks excellent English, Mr. Director, so I'll let her talk for herself. If you have any opening questions, just ask her. Please call her Ludmila."

"Why do you come to the CIA to discuss these matters, Ludmila?" Carlini said. "When somebody seeks immunity, and presumably asylum, the questions are usually directed to the Department of State."

"Because Vasili says he prefers to speak to spies. As a long time KGB man, Vasili thinks that spies are the most trustworthy people to talk to. They know when to keep their mouths shut."

Both Carlini and Buster stifled a laugh.

"Well, I'm glad you and your husband think that way, Ludmila," Carlini said. "We'll try not to disappoint you. You do realize that when you speak to me you're speaking to the United States Government, including the White House? Now please tell us what you know about the *USS Louisiana* and the whereabouts of President Blake."

"My husband, Vasili, was the man in charge of the Russian part of the operation to steal—I think you call it hijack—the American submarine as well as kidnap your president. He can tell you everything about it."

"Why would your husband come to the United States Government?" Carlini asked. "Is there a problem between him and his government?"

"Vasili can explain all of this better than I can, but I can tell you that he, as well as many other Russian officials, are not happy with Boris Chernekov, our new president. They don't trust him. Vasili is a life-long Navy man, as well as a KGB guy. He is used to following orders, but he thinks that the hijacking of your submarine and kidnapping President Blake are both insane actions. Many other people agree with him. He calls President Chernekov a 'crazy scoombag.' "

"When can your husband be here?" Buster asked.

"He can be here tomorrow," Ludmila said. "The naval conference starts the next day."

"Buster, I don't have to tell you how to do it," Carlini said, "but get Admiral Yuschenko to my office under cover of absolute secrecy."

—+ +—

"Dee, it's Bill Carlini. Tomorrow I'm meeting with a man who I think you should talk to."

I was escorted into Carlini's office the next morning. Carlini likes to spring surprises, and I was about to have one sprung on me.

A short stocky man wearing a gray business suit walked into Carlini's office, along with a guy who was introduced as his lawyer, Jack Townsend.

"Good morning, Admiral Yuschenko," Carlini said. "Your wife Ludmila and your attorney have given us a general outline of what we're going to talk about. You've met me, Director of the CIA. This gentlemen is my chief deputy, Agent Akhbar, but we all call him Buster. And this young lady is Mrs. Diana Blake, the wife of the kidnapped president and the current Chief of Staff to President Benton. Ludmila says that you have a lot to tell us. Please do so."

As Yuschenko shook each of our hands, he held mine a bit longer, bent over and kissed it.

"Your photographs show you to be a beautiful woman, Mrs. Blake," Yuschenko said, "but I must admit that in person I find you stunning. Please pardon the ravings of an old romantic."

If nothing else, I found the guy charming in an old school sort of way.

"Thank you for the compliment, Admiral, but I'm not here for flattery as pleasant as it may be. I'm representing the President of the United States. Please tell us why you're here."

"Correction, Mrs. Blake," Admiral Yuschenko said, "You're representing the *acting* president. We will now discuss the real president, your husband. Let me begin by saying that Russia has gone through a major change recently with the coup that overthrew President Vladimir Putin. Our new president, Boris Chernekov is a different sort of man. I shall be blunt. He is a power-hungry maniac. My country suddenly finds itself in an untenable position. We have hijacked one of your nuclear ballistic missile submarines and have kidnaped President Blake."

"Were you not in charge of the operation, Admiral?" I asked.

"Yes, I was. With the benefit of hindsight, I realize that I made a terrible mistake, even if I acted under orders. But if it wasn't me, it would have been someone else. If I refused I would have been killed. Yes, I organized the hijacking, including the fake explosion and release of debris to make it appear the *Louisiana* had sunk. In my heart of hearts I hoped that the operation would soon come to an end, and that it would be nothing more than a way to embarrass the United States. But it is much more than that. My country, which denies any involvement, finds itself on the horns of a dilemma. What can we do with one of your submarines? Of course we can find valuable intelligence and discover secrets of your nuclear program that we didn't know existed. That is exactly what is going on now. A team of engineers is working full time to learn the secrets of the *Louisiana*."

"Where is the *Louisiana*, Admiral?" asked Buster.

"She is at the old underground submarine base at Balaklava on the Crimean Peninsula. President Chernekov has decided to resurrect the old facility and bring it back to life as an active base. I'm going to guess that your satellites didn't notice."

"Why wouldn't we notice?" said Buster, the spook who never shows his hand.

"Did you see a submarine enter the facility last week?" said Yuschenko.

"Why do you ask?" said Carlini. "Was it the *Louisiana*?"

"Yes, it was the *Louisiana*," Yuschenko said. "I admire that the trained spy in you didn't admit it, but I know for a fact that you did not see a submarine. The wonderful thing about the Balaklava facility is that a submarine can enter and exit without surfacing. The *Louisiana* did enter Balaklava and is still there now."

"Where is the President?" I asked, my voice bordering on a shout.

"He is safely in a residence facility on the base, along with Tony Riordan, his Chief of Staff. His quarters are probably comfortable, but I can't be sure. I have been replaced by General Zhukov of the Russian Army. General Zhukov does not hold your president with the respect that I did, but I know for a fact that your husband is still at Balaklava. As of right now, I am 'off-the-case' as you Americans say."

"Admiral Yuschenko," said Bill Carlini, "the major question concerns your plans for both the *Louisiana* and the President. We can see no intelligent strategy to back up the plan. Russia doesn't need one of our nuclear subs—you have your own. And what could you possibly do with the president? The American people, thanks to our free press, believe that President Blake is alive. What could you possibly do with him, other than return him to us immediately?"

"On that point, Mr. Director," Yuschenko said, "I am as much in the dark as you. It doesn't make sense to detain President Blake."

If it doesn't make sense to detain him, I thought to myself, then why the fuck don't you convince Chernekov to release him, you sorry dick? I'm thinking nasty thoughts while trying to appear polite and diplomatic.

"How was the operation pulled off?" Buster asked. "It seems that you couldn't have done it without inside mutineers."

"Captain Joseph Campbell was the chief mutineer," Yuschenko said, "but there were plenty of others. All told, only five people were shot, including two of President Blake's Secret Service people. A lot of Americans helped us to make this happen."

"Is Russia alone in this operation?" I asked.

"That, madam, is the crucial question," Yuschenko said. "The answer is no, Russia is not alone. Many of the American mutineers had been groomed for months. I know very little about them, other than their complicity in the operation."

"Admiral," said Carlini, "let me see if I can summarize all of this. You told us the secrets of how the sub was hijacked and President Blake was kidnapped. But we don't know Russia's intentions for either the sub or the President. And we're still blind as to what will happen. Any suggestions?"

"Mr. Director, I came to your office as a Russian patriot. That's the truth. I want to save my country from any further damage that may be caused by this insane adventure."

"And how can you do that, admiral?" I asked.

"I will be your inside man," Yuschenko said. "I will be your mole, your *spookie.*"

"It's pronounced 'spook,' Admiral," Buster said. "Welcome aboard. I look forward to working with you."

CHAPTER 22

"Agent Akhbar is here to see you, Mrs. Blake."

"Send him in, Barbara."

I'm kind of fanatical about people making appointments. With a crazy position like Chief of Staff to the President, it's the only way to keep order. But I always made an exception for Buster. CIA Director Carlini calls Buster an action figure dressed up like a human being. He's right. When Buster's on the move, work with him, I've learned, otherwise you'll get run over. An unannounced meeting with Buster is never a waste of time. I was surprised to see that he brought Carlini with him.

"I'm guessing that you spookies have something amazing to tell me," I said.

"Yes, it is amazing," Buster said. "We've already met our unexpected ally, our fellow spookie as he calls himself, Admiral Yuschenko. But here's the amazing idea I want to share with you. I have two words I'd like to throw on the table. You may find it shocking, but it's something we've got to think about."

"So what are the two words?" I asked. Buster loves to set the stage for important announcements.

"Bartholomew Martin," Buster said.

I looked at Carlini, who just sat there with his studied poker face.

"You've got to be fucking kidding me, Buster," I said. "Pardon my language, but I thought our former president just disappeared. Last I heard he was in his viper's nest in Kurdistan. What could Martin have to do with any of this?"

"Please keep in mind Dee, that I'm just speculating," Buster said. "But speculation is all we have until we uncover some solid evidence. We all know that Bartholomew Martin is a strange character, maybe the strangest character in American history. Your husband's election put that on display. Martin made an unforgettable scene by never offering his congratulations, and the son of a bitch didn't even show up at the inauguration. We know from his four years in office that he's a power hungry despot. He came close to turning our country into a dictatorship. People like that never go away. Hey, Dee, you're a professor of political science. You know this better than I do. Dictators don't just crawl away and count their money. Once they have power, the only thing in life for them is getting it back. I have absolutely no evidence to support this, but my gut screams at me that Bartholomew Martin may be involved. Remember, he had a large part of the military on his side, and I don't think he enjoys being ex-president."

"Okay, Buster, I got it," I said. "Your logic is on target, even though we have no evidence. So where do we go from here? Do you have plans for getting your people inside?"

"Dee, I'm sure you understand, but there are certain matters that I'm not free to discuss."

"Bullshit," I said, with no attempt to keep my voice low. "You're speaking to the White House. When you talk to me you're talking to President Benton. Tell me about your plans."

"I'm sorry, Dee," Buster said. "You're absolutely correct. Sometimes I forget just who you are. So in answer to your question, yes, we already have people inside, as I'm sure you'd expect, and we have plans to put more insiders in place. Besides our new friend, Spookie Yuschenko, we have spies in Russia, of course, as well as Iran, Syria, Yemen, Saudi Arabia and what's left of Libya. You'll be happy to know that we have three of our people at Martin's compound in Kurdistan. They've been there before he even took office."

"But there's something we haven't spoken about, Buster, and I know that Mrs. Blake wants to know," Director Carlini said. "What's our major suspicion about where the *Louisiana* will show up, not to mention the President?"

"I'm putting my money on Iran," Buster said. "Their new ayatollah, Abad Tavana, is just the kind of messianic nut who would love to have a nuclear ballistic missile sub at his disposal."

"But why would Russia want to facilitate the Iranian nut?" I said. "Why the hell would they go through this elaborate caper in order to turn the sub over to Tehran?"

"Let's not be so sure it's Russia that's facilitating this," Buster said. "My theory is that Bartholomew Martin intends to use Iran as a surrogate to attack the United States."

"Right now, gentlemen," I said, "all we have is questions. Our next job is to find answers."

If Buster's right, where the hell does that leave Matt?

CHAPTER 23

B artholomew Martin, the former President of the United States, sat in his office in Kurdistan with his chief lieutenant, Walter Bingham. His office was in his house, which he designed himself. Adjoining a large den is a patio overlooking a half-acre yard surrounded by fig trees. Off to the right, in an opening between the trees, is a man-made three-acre lake. Judging from the view, you wouldn't know if you were in Kurdistan or Minnesota. Martin is one of the wealthiest men on earth, and among his many possessions are houses around the world.

Martin lost to Matthew Blake in a landslide in the last presidential election. His colleagues in the Freedom from Terror party all agreed that Martin overplayed his hand during his first and only administration. By a blizzard of executive orders, Martin had come close to overturning the United States Constitution and replacing it with a simpler code of law—the law of Bartholomew Martin. Orders from his desk became a daily part of American life for four years. He commanded the freezing of assets, property confiscation, warrantless searches, and an array of orders all aimed toward one goal—to consolidate his power. Martin, for a brief period of time, had become America's first dictator.

On election night, as the mounting evidence of a landslide came through, Bartholomew Martin refused to concede, or even to place a congratulatory call to his opponent, Matt Blake. Breaking with a long tradition, Martin even refused to attend the inauguration of Matt Blake as president. Ever since the transfer of power, Martin had become an obscure figure. He sold his Manhattan penthouse and moved to his other main location, Kurdistan, the seat of power of his group of thugs, who now call themselves *The Reformers.*

"Walter, bring me up to date on the amazing disappearance of the *USS Louisiana* and our esteemed president," Martin said.

"As you know sir, the event would have never happened without our technical help."

"Walter, make certain that this subject is never discussed outside these walls except between you and me," Martin said, his voice uncharacteristically raised. Martin made it a point of pride never to yell.

"Yes, sir," said Bingham. "The information that we've given the Russians on launch procedures and targeting codes have saved them over a year's worth of reengineering. They now have a strategic weapon that can be used. As you know, sir, some of our inside people are submariners themselves."

"But, Walter, you and I know that they don't need another strategic weapon. They have plenty of their own."

"Yes, sir, but as we've discussed," Bingham said, "the Russians now possess the two most powerful trading assets they could ever imagine—the *Louisiana* and President Blake. The sub will eventually find its way into the hands of another country. The only question now is which one."

"Yes, which one is the question, and I am the one who will provide the answer. Now tell me about the suddenly powerless President Blake."

"Our sources tell me that he's being held as a prisoner. He apparently thinks that the United States government believes that the sub was destroyed, along with him."

"How many of our people aboard the sub?"

"20 of our people are crewmembers, including the captain, as well as three engineers."

"And what about the American government, Walter? What do they believe?"

"It's become common thinking, Bartholomew, that the destruction of the *Louisiana* was a deception. The Americans believe that the sub still exists, along with Matthew Blake. The only ones who believe it really was a hijacking are President Blake and his Chief of Staff."

"Perfect. Such a belief provides for all sorts of strategic possibilities. Can you tell me anything about the thinking of Boris Chernekov, Russia's new president? We were in constant communication with him prior to the sub hijacking, but I would like to know what's going on with him now."

"As you well know, Bartholomew, Chernekov is a headstrong man. Some think that he's insane. But as unpredictable as he is, he knows he has a gigantic bargaining chip."

"Yes, he does, Walter, and the good fellow needs guidance on how to use it."

⋙ ⋘

A month later Bartholomew Martin again met with Walter Bingham at his home in Kurdistan.

"So tell me. Walter, how did your meeting with President Chernekov go?"

"I couldn't get anywhere near Chernekov, Bartholomew, even though he said the he would personally meet me when I made the appointment. I was shuffled off to one of his aides. From the man's mannerisms and demeanor, I could see that he was a low-level assistant. He had no authority to speak, and he didn't seem to know what I was talking about. My trip was a waste of time, I'm afraid."

"No, Walter, it was not a waste of time. Consider it part of your education. You now know more about Boris Chernekov than you did before."

"How do you suggest that I proceed, Bartholomew? Try to make another appointment and hope for the best?"

"No, that would be senseless, Walter. Chernekov has a well-earned reputation as someone who likes to keep people running in circles. I want you to find me the name of a senior official who speaks with authority and I will meet with him myself. Because I'm no longer a head of state, Chernekov would never meet with me. I'm surprised that he even agreed to meet you, even though he had no intention of keeping the appointment."

"But, Bartholomew, won't it compromise your position if you met personally with a high official. You will not have that wonderful thing called 'deniability.' If you're asked a question, you'll be expected to answer it. You can't go back later and say your aide misspoke. But if you meet the official yourself, it will be you who's doing the speaking."

"Walter, whether I'm speaking, shouting, or jumping up and down, I believe we have the evidence to get the attention of Chernekov himself. As we've discussed, Walter, Boris Chernekov is a madman. The Cold War was never hot enough for him. He's an unreformed communist, but his goals point more toward gathering power, no matter what the ideology. He has a few pet projects, one of which is to resurrect the old Soviet Union. He wants nothing more than to see Russia as the head of a vast empire. He actually believes that, under his leadership, people will happily go back to the days of the Soviet Union. Educating youth is one of Chernekov's biggest goals. He sees the younger generations as the future of the new Soviet state. In his brief tenure in power he has formed hundreds of 'youth brigades,' bringing together children for mass indoctrination. It reminds me of the Hitler Youth. He prides himself on his almost religious dedication to protecting youth from corruption of any sort, sexual or otherwise. If you and I didn't know better we could mistake him for a stodgy old preacher."

"Of course our evidence shows otherwise, Bartholomew. We know that he's a fraud, that he's a child molester, a serial rapist of young boys, and we know how to expose him, including photographs."

"Not only will we expose him, Walter. We have enough proof to bring down his government. Then we shall see who determines the destiny of the *USS Louisiana* and its famous crew member."

CHAPTER 24

"Brace yourself, Ali, but I think that the source of the hijacking and kidnapping conspiracy may be a lot closer to America itself. One of my contacts thinks that the former American president, Bartholomew Martin, may be involved."

"My God, Basim," Behzadi said, "Bartholomew Martin, America's first dictator. I was happy when the American voters turned him out of office in a landslide election. Just another reason for my fondness for America. Is this man still active?"

"As you know, Ali, Martin virtually disappeared from sight after the election. He didn't call President Blake to concede the election, and he didn't even appear at the inauguration in January. Bartholomew Martin now spends his time in Kurdistan at the compound of his new group. They call themselves *The Reformers*. My friend thinks that Martin may be involved in the submarine and kidnapping plot."

"I've never seen the world so unstable," Behzadi said, "and that is because of unstable leaders. Russia is now headed by Boris Chernekov, a tyrannical thug. We are led by Abad Tavana, a religious fanatic and tyrant. Now you tell me that the insane American, Bartholomew Martin, may be involved. And how do you think Iran may be a part of this? Our fearless leader, Tavana, is obsessed with punishing the Great Satan. I don't know how, but I'm sure Iran will be part of this plot. Just how we would be involved is just speculation, but whoever planned the event won't be content to let the submarine sit idle or to leave President Blake unscathed. I fear that we are just beginning to see the early parts of this strange plot. Bartholomew Martin is a man given to conniving and plotting. I'm sure that he sees our crazy leader as a man who can be manipulated by his own wild fantasies. I believe that Bartholomew Martin intends to use Iran for his own purposes, just as he used his own people when he was President of the United States."

CHAPTER 25

Oh my God, I miss Matt. My theory about the submarine plot is now the theory of the United States Government—the *Louisiana* still exists and Matt's alive. But that theory doesn't replace his being next to me. And the theory doesn't explain a lot of shit. We still have an enormous amount of unanswered questions, like what do they intend to do with Matt, and how are they treating him. And most important of all—how the hell are we going to free him?

"Agent Akhbar is here to see you, Mrs. Blake."

Buster walked in. I've known him long enough to tell from the expression on his face that he had something important to say. His spook self would cringe at the idea that I can read him from his facial expression. Buster prides himself on anonymity. I pride myself on observation. He thinks his poker face throws everybody off. I can tell when he's got nothing or a full house.

"So tell me, my brilliant spook, what is your current thinking?"

"My thinking, Dee," Buster said, "and I've gone over this with Bill Carlini countless times, is that Bartholomew Martin is about to use Iran as his surrogate in declaring war on the United States.

Martin would never be so stupid to think that his band of hoods could pull such a thing off by themselves. No, I'm convinced that he wants to use the *Louisiana* and President Blake to do what he can't do alone."

"Do you expect them to move the *Louisiana*—and Matt—to Iran?"

"That's the inescapable conclusion, Dee. It lets Russia off the hook and brings the *End of Days* and Ayatollah Tavana's prayed-for conflagration of the West closer. It make ultimate sense to have the *Louisiana* docked in Iran."

"Any idea where in Iran they plan to make the move?" I asked.

"It could be any Iranian naval base," Buster said, "but we're concentrating on Bandar Abbas, the main facility of the Iranian Navy. The base is located on the Strait of Hormuz on the Persian Gulf. It can accommodate large ships which will be useful if they think a defensive battle is necessary. The surrounding area is flat and defensible."

"Buster, I know this is just in the early stage, but give me an idea of how we plan to attack."

"Yes, Dee, it is in the early stages, but here is our current thinking. Once we get a fix on the president's location, we'll send in a company of SEALs to secure his safety, and back that up with hundreds of aerial strikes launched from our carriers in the Gulf. We'll infiltrate the *Louisiana* with some of our people who are trained in operating a submarine, because one of our objectives will be to secure and remove the sub. We'll position surface ships and attack subs nearby to provide support. But our primary objective is to insure that President Blake is safely removed from danger. If necessary, once we have your husband in our safe custody, we'll attack and sink the *Louisiana* by aerial bombardment and torpedoes. That's only if we're unable to capture it ourselves."

"Buster, how do you feel about these plans? Frankly, they scare the living shit out of me."

"I'll be honest with you, Dee, which is the only way the two of us communicate. It scares me too. The SEALs are the best fighters on earth, but we're talking about a very fluid operating theater. We'll be vastly outnumbered, which is a familiar scenario for a SEAL operation. An open field battle is not in the SEAL vocabulary. But it won't be an easy mission. The president is your husband, and he's also my Commander in Chief. We're all on the same page. Don't worry, Dee, we'll get POTUS the hell out of there."

"I admire your fighting spirit, Buster, but I remind you that we don't even know where 'there' is. Do we have any inside people on the *Louisiana*?"

"I remind myself that when I'm talking to you, Dee, I'm talking to the White House. So, as much as it horrifies me as a spook to say this, the answer to your question is 'yes.' We do have inside people, three to be exact, aboard the *Louisiana*."

"And we freely communicate back and forth with these people?" I asked.

"Yes, Dee, I talk to a Marine Captain named Mike Conklin. He's our agent in charge."

So Buster has a plan, one that involves guns, rockets, and bombs. And in the middle of all that shit will be Matt—*my Matt.*

CHAPTER 26

I rigged a comfortable blindfold to shield me from the garish light bulb. It wasn't tight, more like a bandana loosely draped over my forehead. I resumed my time-keeping routine of exercise, the Gettysburg Address, and meditation. Adjusting from my time in total darkness, I estimated that I'd been in solitary for 10 days. My mind kept wandering to Dee, and I did nothing to stop it. Just like the woman herself, the thought of her calmed me. The thought that she thinks of herself as a widow did not calm me.

A gentle knock on the door grabbed my attention. It was not the full-frontal intrusion of General Zhukov with his jingling medals, a sound I'd learned to expect.

"Good morning, Mr. President," Petty Officer Jackson said. He carried a tray of food.

"Looks like we have a new chef," I said. Scrambled eggs, home fried potatoes, and ham, along with rye toast. Something has obviously changed, I thought.

"I was expecting to see my favorite conversationalist, General Zhukov," I said.

"General Zhukov had an accident, sir. His body was found floating a few yards from the *Louisiana* this morning. He seems to have slipped and hit his head."

"If you slip and bang your head, a splash of water in the face is usually enough to revive you. I'm surprised that it killed him, the poor man."

"The right side of his skull was bashed in by a large blunt object," sir.

"What a pity," I said. "I'll have to send my condolences to the family."

I've thought of Petty Officer Jackson as a friend, sort of. Compared to the recently departed General Zhukov, a rattlesnake would look like a friend. This morning's conversation nailed it. Could this sailor really be an ally, not a mutineer?

"Sir, your quarters are about to be moved. You're going back to the *Louisiana*, along with Mr. Riordan, your Chief of Staff. I can't say any more."

Leaving this rat hole is one of the few pleasures I've allowed myself to contemplate. But why are we going back to the sub? I'd find out shortly.

CHAPTER 27

Three men entered my compartment and blindfolded me—not with my comfortable light-dousing blindfold, but a full head covering. Before wrapping my head, one of the men told me to gather my belongings. Didn't take long—my toothbrush, toothpaste, and the can opener that I used to mark time.

As they escorted me up the brow to the sub I wondered why the hell a blindfold was necessary. Could someone be worried that I could identify the *Louisiana*?

Once aboard, they took me to my new quarters. One of the men removed my head covering. I immediately recognized the compartment as the same one that I occupied before.

"Please make yourself at home, sir," said one of my handlers in perfect English. He gave me a mug of fresh brewed coffee.

"Is the prisoner secured?" came a shout from outside my room.

A tall fit man wearing Marine fatigues walked into my space. He was about six-feet, had close- cropped square haircut, blue eyes, and the martial bearing of a typical Marine.

"You are now my prisoner," he said loudly as he seated himself. "You will speak when spoken to, and not before. Any interaction you have with a crewmember will be directly through me. Do I make myself understood?"

Great, I thought, a General Zhukov with a Midwestern accent.

"Yes, Captain, quite understood."

He stood and checked the lock on the door. When he returned to his seat, he spoke softly.

"Buster sends his regards, Mr. President."

I dropped the mug and spilled coffee all over the table.

"Are you saying that you communicate with Buster, aka Gamal Akhbar?"

"To get right to the point Mr. President, I'm a mole, Buster's hand-picked insider. I'm on your side, sir."

People know me as a man who's quick with words. But I had no words. I sat and stared at Captain Conklin.

"Another thing, sir. The First Lady sends her love."

Of all the crazy shit I've been through since the *Louisiana* was captured, I had my first feeling of hope. For Dee to send her love meant that she knew I was alive. Obviously Buster would have told her about my mole friend, Captain Conklin.

"Did Buster communicate the First Lady's message, Captain?"

"No sir, she told me herself. President—*acting* President—Benton—has appointed your wife as his Chief of Staff. She told Buster, with the power of the White House behind her, that she wanted to give you a personal communication, and that she'd do it through me. Buster went crazy, of course. As a super spook he has a firm rule that only he should speak directly to a mole. But your wife didn't ask—she *told* him. She's one tough lady, Mr. President."

"So people think I'm alive, and that the *Louisiana* was not sunk? My wife doesn't think she's a widow?"

"Sir, it's an open secret in the States that the sinking of the *Louisiana* was an elaborate ploy. Your wife is a hell of an expert on submarines. She saw through the plot from the beginning. Buster said that she kept telling everybody, 'don't trust the evidence,' a rule she learned from you. After the phony explosion, another sub released hundreds of pieces of 'debris' to convince the world that the *Louisiana* had blown up. It didn't convince your wife. As Buster told me, she referred to the debris field as a 'bullshit yard sale.' "

That's Dee. I could almost hear her saying the words.

"What are the plans, Captain? What's next?" I asked.

"Sir, I'm one part of a big machine. I know what I know, and as you understand from CIA policy, 'need to know' is the doctrine that rules the day. It's the time honored way of keeping a secret just that, a secret. Of course, as President of the United States, your need to know surpasses everybody else's. I tell you in all honesty, sir, that I have no idea what the immediate plans are for the *Louisiana* and yourself. I have a hunch that our government doesn't know either. I'm in communication with Washington, but we don't have much to communicate right now. Mr. President, you know our government better than I do, so I think we both know that plans are in the making to launch a rescue operation and get you the hell out of here. I must be going, sir. You and I can meet for only short periods of time. Keeping my identity secret is the key to all future operations. When I speak to you publicly I will occasionally use harsh words to emphasize that you're my prisoner. But make no mistake, sir, you are my Commander in Chief, and I'm part of a team that intends to reinstall you in the Oval Office."

There was a knock on the door.

"There's someone here to see you," Conklin said.

Tony Riordan walked into my room. I hadn't heard anything about him for weeks. For all I knew he could have been dead.

We threw protocol aside and hugged.

"You look a hell of a lot thinner than the last time I saw you, Tony. Been watching your weight?"

"Yes, sir, I've been watching it disappear. You look quite slim yourself, sir. Cold beets and potatoes does wonders for one's waistline."

I brought my index finger to my lips to indicate 'silence.' Tony and I then checked for bugs. In spite of my conversation with Captain Conklin, I've learned to be paranoid in the past few weeks.

"No doubt about it, Tony, the General Zhukov diet seems to work," I said.

"Have you seen that sadistic bastard recently, Mr. President?"

"I guess you haven't heard. Zhukov has been whacked and tossed into the water. I'm afraid we missed the memorial service. Please remind me to send flowers to the family."

"I haven't heard anything about that, Mr. President. All I know is that we're back on the *Louisiana*. With Zhukov dead, I guess that changes things."

"Yes, a lot of things have changed," I said. "Let me bring you up to speed. We're still prisoners, but we have friends on the inside—deep inside. What I'm about to tell you are things that we have to whisper about."

"Holy shit. We're no longer alone?" Tony said.

"Not even close to being alone. Have you met Mike Conklin, the Marine Captain?"

"He's the guy who showed me into your room. We didn't meet, but I saw his name and rank on his uniform."

"Well, Conklin is the most important man in our lives right now. He's an inside mole, hand-picked by none other than Buster the spook."

"When do I get to meet Conklin, Mr. President?"

"He's a typical spy, Tony. He only comes out of the shadows when he thinks it's necessary. Don't approach him. He'll contact you at the appropriate time, and he's the guy who decides when it's appropriate."

⌐←+ +⌐→

"Has Captain Conklin been in touch with you, Dee?" President Benson asked.

"Yes sir. He called me this morning," I said. "I spoke to Buster in detail about Conklin, and I'm convinced that we're dealing with a real professional spy. If Buster thinks the guy's good, he's definitely good. From everything Buster told me, and from my conversation with Mike Conklin this morning, I think we're dealing with the right guy. One thing bothers me though. Conklin said he has no idea where the *Louisiana* will be headed and no idea of its course."

"Can't Conklin monitor the sub's position and keep us updated?" President Benton asked.

"I wish it were that simple, Mr. President. According to Conklin, all navigational tracking has been disabled and information on the sub's position and course is limited to a select few people. Conklin isn't one of them."

"Then we'll establish a sonar track of the *Louisiana* as soon as Conklin tells us it left Balaklava. Once we get a track on her we won't let go."

"Once again we have a problem, Mr. President," I said. "Conklin told me that they're going to rig the sub to run deep and run silent. As you and I know, the *Louisiana* is one of the stealthiest submarines in the world. It will be difficult to track even with another one of our subs."

"The *Louisiana* may be stealthy but we were able to get three of our people aboard without notice." Benton said. "We've even been in touch with your husband. With three spies aboard, I'd say we're perfectly situated. And remember, Admiral Spookie Yuschenko is on our side."

⇥ ⇤

"Prepare to dive... dive." the public address system announced. The sub took a sudden deep dive at a 45 degree angle.

"Holy shit" I shouted to Tony. "Are these clowns practicing to be cowboys?"

A half hour later Captain Conklin appeared. "I hope you gentlemen enjoyed the ride," Conklin said.

"Is this something new?" I asked.

"Yes, sir, it is," said Conklin. "The captain has decided to abandon secrecy and let all of his crew members in on the plans. Of course he doesn't realize that three people, including myself, are not on his side. Unfortunately I didn't have time to alert you and Tony, Mr. President. He just announced the dive without advance warning."

"So what are these acrobatics all about? We dove almost straight down." I said.

"The objective is to run silent and deep, and to go deep as quickly as possible, Mr. President. Our destination is the Iranian Navy Base at Bandar Abbas, the main base of the Iranian Navy. It's located on the Strait of Hormuz on the Persian Gulf."

"How busy is the Strait?" I asked.

"Quite busy Mr. President. An average of 14 tankers a day pass through the strait carrying 17 million barrels of crude oil."

"We have no idea what they're planning for me and Tony Riordan, is that correct?"

"That's correct Mr. President. We don't want to risk exposing our mole operation by making too many inquiries. Of course I'll alert our government from time to time about you and Mr. Riordan."

He handed Tony and me two Colt 45 pistols with two extra magazines.

"I hope you won't have to use these," Conklin said, "but you both know how."

"We're set to tie up at Bandar Abbas in a half hour, Mr. President," Conklin said. "I've alerted Washington that you and Tony Riordan are now in Iran. Things are about to get interesting."

CHAPTER 28

In the weeks leading up to this, my emotional state has gone from frightened to panic. But now it's different, it's coming to a head. To know that Matt will soon be in the middle of bullets flying scares the living shit out of me. Matt's a hard-nosed and highly decorated Marine who saw a lot of combat, and Tony's no wilting lily either. But bullets don't ask to see your resume—they just come screaming at you.

"Mr. President, I just spoke to Mike Conklin," I said to Rolly Benton. "Things are coming to a head. The *Louisiana* is heading toward the Iranian Navy Base at Bandar Abbas. She should tie up in about a half hour."

"Dee, we're about to enter the next phase of our operation, and it's not going to be pleasant."

I'd never known Rolly Benton to look so shaken. In his long military career he's encountered a lot of painful operations, but this one seemed especially difficult for him. He's about to launch an operation to rescue the President of the United States. Failure could mean not only the loss of the president's life—my husband's life—it could also mean war. Rolly is as tough as nails, but his humanity was showing. How was *I* doing? I looked down at my hands on my lap. I had just shredded another napkin.

"We're about to have a visitor, Dee. Commander Dwight Baxter is in command of the Navy SEAL team that will carry out the rescue mission. He's going to brief us on the details of the operation."

⇒⊩ ⊩⇐

"Mr. President, Madam Chief of Staff, I'd like to introduce Commander Dwight Baxter of the United States Navy," the President's secretary said." She escorted Baxter into the Oval Office, where he came to attention and saluted.

Baxter stood at about 5'11" and had the build of a wrestler.

From everything I've read and heard about Navy SEALs, you want them on your side. SEALs are legendary as a unique fighting force. SEAL is an acronym for Sea, Air and Land. The training, known as BUD/S (Basic Underwater Demolition/SEAL) is the most demanding military preparedness in the world, consisting of six months of grueling physical and mental stress. During "hell week," SEALs spend their time swimming in cold water, crawling through mud, climbing trees and tall obstacles, and jumping out of airplanes from impossible heights like 30,000 feet. All of this is accomplished with little sleep. About 30 percent of those who start SEAL training finish. That means that 70 percent wash out. There is no other way of saying it; SEALs are tough. They are not only professional class athletes, they're also mentally disciplined and intelligent. The idea behind SEAL training is to cheat reality of its surprises. When a SEAL is lying in a pool of mud and cold water, having not eaten for 24 hours, with two hours sleep, surrounded by a superior enemy force, he has one thought: "Been here, done this."

Commander Baxter is a typical SEAL. With his can-do attitude and athletic body, Baxter was ready for anything an enemy may throw against him. After two tours in Iraq and one in Afghanistan, he was a hardened combat veteran.

All of this knowledge should make me feel better, but I'm still scared out of my mind for Matt. I wish I was there personally. I'm good with a pistol and I'd be happy to personally blow the brains out of any scumbag who laid a fucking finger on my Matt. Now what the hell am I doing, going through self-induced fantasies? Calm down. It's time not only to act like an adult, it's time to think like one too.

Baxter and his men had never before been on a mission to rescue their commander in chief. When I considered that the mission would be conducted in a submarine, my stomach did a back flip.

President Benton and I stood to greet our visitor.

"Commander Baxter," said the president, "The mission we're about to discuss is one of the most important military operations the United States has ever launched. We've never been in a position where one of our submarines was hijacked and the president kidnapped. Your job is to put me out of my job and return President Blake to this office."

Rolly walked up to Baxter and reverted to his prior role as a SEAL commander himself. He brought his face within two inches of Baxter's, and looked him in the eyes.

"Failure is not an option, Commander," Rolly said.

"I'm sure you're also aware," I said, "that President Blake is my husband. But your commander in chief is President Benton. You will take orders from him. Now please brief the President and me on your plans."

Baxter stood ram-rod straight.

"Mr. President, Chief of Staff Blake, I'm not going to minimize the complexity and danger of this operation," Baxter said. "Our primary objective is to rescue President Blake. Secondly, we aim to recapture the *USS Louisiana*. We're going to try to accomplish our objectives with minimum loss of life or injuries to our people.

Twenty-five SEALs will be involved, all of whom have had extensive experience with hostage operations. Two of our people speak fluent Farsi, the most widely spoken Persian language. Fifteen men speak Russian, the language of the people who pulled off the hijacking. All of them will wear Russian uniforms. We owe our thanks to the good graces of Admiral Yuschenko, the man who actually planned the hijacking, and has since came over to our side. Yuschenko's a brave guy. He'll be part of our operation, and the most valuable insider we've got for this mission."

"Commander Baxter," President Benton said, "there's something you need to keep in mind. I want you to impress this on the minds of the others as well. And here it is: We're running the risk of nuclear war with Iran. They can't possibly win, but with the 16 active nuclear missiles aboard the *Louisiana*, we could lose over a million Americans."

"I'm well aware of that, sir. We've been training on a nuclear sub for a month."

"When will your team be ready to go, commander?" I asked.

"In exactly eight days, Mrs. Blake. We're going through our final drills at the New London submarine base now."

"Does the operation have a code name," asked the President.

"Yes sir," Baxter said. "We're calling it operation Tango in honor of President Blake's code name."

"You've *got* to be fucking kidding me," I loudly observed. "Why don't you call it Operation Matt Blake? Can't you pick a name that nobody will recognize in the event it's accidentally leaked?"

I realized that my vulgarity, not to mention my shouting, was inappropriate, so I apologized to Baxter and the President. But I did get their attention. I wouldn't have been surprised if, in honor of me, they called it "Operation Foulmouth."

"The alternate name of the mission is 'Operation Springtime,' so we'll go with that," Baxter said. "Much better," I said. "That name is meaningless, and therefore more appropriate. If we went with the original name of the mission—Operation Tango—we may as well call it 'Operation Rescue the President.'"

The President handed me a glass of water. Commander Baxter turned beet red. I guess all of his training and combat experience didn't prepare him for somebody like me. I took a gulp of water and apologized again. I really have to watch my vulgar language.

Fuck it. I'll think about that later.

CHAPTER 29

SEAL platoon X-Rray Bravo is part of Naval Special Warfare Group (NSWG) One, stationed in Coronado, California. The platoon consists of two officers and 14 enlisted men. Platoon X-Ray Bravo trained alongside platoon Yankee Zulu which had the same configuration of officers and enlisted men. Platoon Yankee Zulu was the backup, emphasizing President Benton's command that "failure is not an option." The entire operation was under the command of Commander Baxter, who would accompany the first platoon to go into action.

Both platoons transferred from Coronado, California to New London, Connecticut to train aboard the *USS Pennsylvania*, SSBN 735, an Ohio Class boat similar to the *USS Louisiana*.

The *Pennsylvania* consisted of 15 officers and 140 enlisted personnel, all of whom were replaced with the 32 members of SEAL Platoons X-Ray Bravo and Yankee Zulu, as well as 123 SEALs from other units of Naval Special Warfare Group One. Because of the extreme Top Secret nature of the mission, the status of the new crew as SEALs was not disclosed to anyone, including the regular crew of the sub. The sailors and officers who the SEALs replaced were simply given new orders. Enough members of the SEALs were experienced in the operation of a submarine to make up an operational crew once the *Pennsylvania* (and later, hopefully, the *Louisiana*) got underway.

One month prior to the launch of the rescue mission the entire crew of the *Pennsylvania* consisted of SEALs.

The training aboard the *USS Pennsylvania* began one month before the planned launch of Operation Springtime. The most intensive preparations were done by the two platoons assigned to the mission. The first part of the training was for each SEAL to memorize every compartment on the sub and its code number. After that, the exercise broke down into "scenarios." One scenario called for violent resistance by the "enemy," another partial resistance, and a third, no resistance at all. They drilled heavily for scenario one, violent resistance. A key part of their training had to do with using firearms on a submarine. In a submerged sub, despite its solid construction, the men had to avoid shooting wildly and risk hitting a pipe or electronic instrument.

Thanks to Captain Conklin, the platoon knew the exact location of President Blake and Tony Riordan. The SEALs concentrated intense training on protecting the corridor leading up to the President's suite.

Another area that received careful attention was *Sherwood Forest*, the compartment that housed the ICBMs and their controls. The most critical part of the mission was to rescue President Blake, and closely following that in the list of importance was securing the missile compartment.

The post-training plan called for the SEALs to board a Boeing C-17 Globemaster at Hanscom Air Force Base in Massachusetts. They would be flown to Hamad International Airport in Qatar.

From there they would board ground transportation in the early morning hours to waiting boats on the Persian Gulf. The two platoons would travel separately to provide redundancy in the event that something went wrong.

CHAPTER 30

I sat in the White House Situation Room with the President, CIA Director Bill Carlini, Buster, and about every electronic device ever invented.

On my way I picked up a fresh supply of napkins for shredding.

The President had just taken a call, one of many, from Russian Admiral Yuschenko, who had turned from our enemy to one of our best allies. We all refer to him as "Spookie," because he once mispronounced the word "spook." It stuck with him as a nickname.

"Spookie just advised me that he has been in touch with the *Louisiana*'s new command, and he knows the course the sub will take," President Benton said.

Commander Baxter took personal command of SEAL platoon X-Ray Bravo. This command would normally be handled by a more junior officer, but Baxter was well aware of the stakes in this mission.

"I've been in situations like this before, a clandestine op ready to take off," said the President. "The only thing that ever makes it bearable is my knowledge of the SEALs. They're not only tough, they're also smart." He turned to me and said, "You're new to this, Dee. Just stay focused. We're going to win this thing."

"*This thing* includes my husband's life, Mr. President. Pardon me if I seem a bit edgy."

I realized I was being out of line, but I felt as if I was standing on the edge of a tall building with a strong wind at my back. I was scared shitless.

"Buster, let the video roll," the President said. Commander Baxter and two other SEALs had a live videocam on their chests. It's as if we were watching a movie—a horror movie.

"Dee, it's perfectly understandable if you want to leave the room," said Rolly. "We're about to watch this operation unfold in real time."

"No, sir, I'll stay," I said. "Matt is going through this in real time. The least I can do is be with him in real time, if only on video."

I can sound tough when I want to, but my words only masked my feeling of near panic. I held my knees with both hands to mask the trembling. We watched and heard Captain Boris Petrov, the new Russian commander of the *Louisiana*, order the boat to get underway. Next to him stood Captain Joseph Campbell, the treasonous former captain of the *Louisiana*. Petrov explained to his assistant that he wanted to run the sub through its paces to prepare for a long range cruise.

When the sub leveled off at its pre-determined depth, Petrov commanded, "Steer course 230."

The video zoomed to Petrov's head. As we watched, a gun suddenly come into view, aimed at Petrov. Behind him we could see another officer with a gun at his head.

"Put your hands behind your back," we heard a SEAL say, "If you make any sudden move, the last thing you feel will be a bullet entering your brain."

We heard distant shouts with American accents. Others were in Farsi or Russian. Another video picked up the scene in the wardroom, the officers' dining room. Seven of the ten men present had their hands behind their backs. Two of the three SEALs held guns on them, while the third placed them in handcuffs. The next video scene was back in the control room where we could see Captain Petrov and three handcuffed officers.

"Notice, Dee, that this operation is choreographed like a Broadway show." The President's commentary did nothing for my screaming stomach.

"Maybe we should all break out into song and dance," I said, my sarcastic mouth on full display. I can be totally insubordinate when I'm scared. I mumbled an apology as President Rolly chuckled. At least poor Commander Baxter wasn't there for me to abuse.

We watched the control room as a Russian sailor reached inside his uniform and came out with a gun. His head exploded in front of us as one of the SEALs opened fire.

"As I said, Dee, we're watching this in real time," the President said. It freaked me out to see specks of blood on the camera lens.

"All stations report," Commander Baxter shouted into his microphone. One by one, a total of five men were required to report his status, such as, "Station three secure," or "Station five on alert." Until all stations reported as secure, Baxter knew the operation wasn't over. Even after all stations reported positively, it was necessary to fan out to arrest stragglers, an operation known as 'mopping up' I was told. I recalled the blood specks on the video lens.

"Director Carlini, Buster, you guys did a great job with intelligence. Our guys know exactly who to arrest," President Benton said.

The next video scene focused in on Captain Joseph Campbell, former commanding officer of the *Louisiana* and head mutineer. He was sitting handcuffed to a chair. Captain Conklin was standing next to him.

"Joseph Campbell," Conklin said, "I won't address you by your military rank because you no longer have one. You are under arrest for treason. You have a right to keep your mouth shut unless I ask you a specific question. If you don't wish to exercise that right I'll blow your fucking treasonous head off."

We all looked at President Benton, who said: "Traitors don't follow the Geneva Convention, but this situation is murky. It looks like I'm going to be exercising my 'pardon pen' for Captain Conklin after this operation."

"Why don't you let him blow the bastard's head off first," I said. "That would make it worth your while to pardon him." The thought occurred to me that I was turning into a plain mean bitch. So what?

A SEAL held up a grease board for Baxter to look at. We could see that he was tapping a spot on the board.

"Station Two report," shouted Baxter. There was no response. He turned to five SEALs who were standing by to assist. "Go to Station Two and secure it. Advise me immediately as to your progress."

"Dear God," said Buster.

"Why the sudden prayer?" the President asked.

"Station Two is also known as *Sherwood Forest*, the compartment where the missiles are housed, along with their primary controls," Buster said. "Unless those guys can secure that station, we'll have one live boomer with 16 missiles to worry about. Until Station Two is secure, America will be in the crosshairs."

We could hear rapid gunfire. The video focused on *Sherwood Forest*. Three bodies lay on the deck, none wearing a SEAL uniform. Commander Bill Gillespie came into view. He was the newly appointed weapons officer for the *Louisiana*.

"Commander Gillespie is here to check on the missiles," said Petty Officer Petrone, the SEAL with the videocam. We watched as Gillespie went from silo to silo. The camera was set on speaker so Baxter could communicate directly with Gillespie.

"Whatta you got commander?" Baxter asked.

"We got the flames of hell about to be unleashed in 15 minutes," Gillespie said. "All of the nukes are armed. They'll launch at five minute intervals. From what Captain Conklin told me, all are targeted against East Coast cities in the States."

"This is President Benton," Rolly said into the microphone. "Patch me into Commander Gillespie."

"Gillespie here, sir."

"Commander, how could the missiles be armed without my code? I put in the changes this morning."

"The simple answer, sir, is that I don't know. The codes appear to have been manually reset."

"Mr. President," I said, "If you recall, CNO Patterson was worried that the firing codes could be changed to manual. It looks like that's what happened."

"Get me President Blake," Baxter said to his aide. "Ask him to come here to the control room." He looked into the camera and said, "I don't have any training or background for this situation, Mr. President. I've determined that *both* of our presidents should communicate on this one."

Matt walked into the control room surrounded by SEALs. My God, he's lost weight, I thought, but he still looks wonderful.

"Good morning, Dee," he said. As simple as that – "Good morning, Dee." How can he be so casual? We haven't seen each other in weeks and we thought we may never be together again, and all the hell he has to say is 'good morning.' Then I realized something. Matt's in a situation that is still potentially explosive. Here I am, nowhere near danger, and I expect him to say sweet nothings to me over a video feed. Snap out of it, I thought to myself. I just saw my Matt being Matt—calm under pressure.

"Get back here as soon as you can, honey, so we can jump into bed and screw our brains out." Of course I didn't say that. But I did think it. What I said was, "Wow, you lost weight. I guess the food wasn't too good."

This situation is getting so weird it should be done in a cartoon. Everybody on the *Louisiana* is sitting on 16 armed nuclear missiles, and Matt and I are shooting the shit like we're in a grocery store.

"Mr. President," Matt said.

"The name's Rolly, sir," said President Benton.

"Well my name's Matt as you well know. Now that we've gotten that out of the way, please tell me what's going on that I don't already know about."

"Bottom line, Matt, your weapons officer just confirmed that all 16 of the *Louisiana*'s missiles are armed and one has begun its countdown to launch. I believe that Captain Conklin has told you about the change in arming procedures. They were manually armed and are targeted toward American cities. The first is set to launch in 15 minutes and each will take off at five minute intervals after that."

"Rolly, what kind of assets do we have anywhere near the *Louisiana*?" Matt asked.

"We have two frigates and two attack subs within five miles of you. I've already ordered them to converge on the *Louisiana*'s position."

"Okay, here's the plan," said Matt, "but let me know what you think first, Rolly. You're still the President. We need to off-load all personnel onto the two frigates and get them the hell out of here. If my submarine knowledge is as good as Dee taught me, we can dive the *Louisiana* by remote control. Is Commander Gillespie there?"

"Gillespie here, Mr. President."

"From what I just learned," Matt said, "the nukes were manually armed. Is there any way to disarm them?"

"Sir, except for the one that has begun its countdown, I think I can disarm the others."

"You *think*, commander?" Matt said. "Can you give me something more solid to go on?"

"Yes, sir, I can disarm the other 15 nukes."

"Well, Rolly," Matt said, "Our problem is significantly less than it was a few minutes ago. We need to disarm the remaining 15 nukes, and dive the sub with the one that's ticking. But we still have a problem with the missile that's counting down. It will be one huge explosion deep under the sea. Dee, are you there?"

"I'm here, Mr. President." I can't believe I called Matt Mr. President, but the tension of the situation seemed to call for formality.

"Dee, does anything I've said make sense? You've become a submarine expert in the past few weeks. Tell me if the plan fits together."

"It does make sense Mr. President—Matt. The critical element is time. After we dive the sub, it will implode when it hits a depth of 2,400 feet. I have no idea what that will do for the firing mechanism on the ticking missile. We need to have the surface ships and the attack subs out of there. One thing we don't know. If the missile that's ticking explodes from water pressure, will it set off explosions of the other missiles? That would make for one big nasty neighborhood."

⊷⊹⊶

Mike Conklin left the control room abruptly, telling Commander Baxter that he'd be right back. He returned five minutes later, accompanied by a handcuffed Captain Petrov, the former Russian commander of the *Louisiana.*

"What's up, Mike?" Matt said to Conklin.

"Captain Petrov," said Conklin, "tell these people what you told me. *Now.*"

"I am not political. I am a patriotic man who loves his country. I have a wife and four children. I'm a sailor and an engineer."

"I didn't ask you for a fucking autobiography. Talk to us about your engineering experience, Captain," Conklin said with a handgun pointed at Petrov's head. "To be blunt, are you familiar with the arming mechanism for the ballistic missiles?"

"Yes," said Petrov. "I helped to design the new protocols. I know how to arm and disarm a ballistic missile."

"Let's take Captain Petrov to *Sherwood Forest*," Baxter said. They left the control room along with six SEALs.

"Zoom in on them, Mike," President Benton said. "We want to see what's going on."

We all watched as Captain Petrov pressed buttons and turned dials.

"This missile was not only armed," said Petrov, "but its timer was set. It is now inert. The others will take a total of a few minutes—plenty of time."

The release of psychological pressure on the *Louisiana* as well as the White House was palpable. It was as if you looked up and saw a piano falling and about to hit you, when, at the last moment, you stepped out of the way. The operation was a complete success—we had the *Louisiana* back and soon I'd have my Matt.

"I just placed a quick phone call to Chief Justice Roberts, President Matt," said Rolly Benton. "I told him to dust off the 25th Amendment and to prepare to administer an oath. I recommend, sir that you take the oath immediately where you are, and the chief justice can do it ceremoniously when you return to Washington. As you know the Constitution doesn't specify who can administer the oath. Remember that Calvin Coolidge took the oath from his father, a notary public, after the death of President Harding."

"Hey, Rolly," Matt said, "you're not dead, last I checked, and therefore it's not an emergency. The transfer can take place when I get to Washington."

Among other things, Matt is also a gentleman.

CHAPTER 31

President Benton ordered Air Force One to meet Matt and Tony Riordan in London, their last stop on the way home. It would be too slow, all agreed, for Matt to return on the *Louisiana*. Of course the plane won't be known officially as Air Force One until Matt is sworn in. Plans had to be made quickly, so Matt will take the oath in the House of Representatives chamber in the Capitol Building, the room where the president gives the State of the Union Address every year.

—<+ +>—

Along with a massive group of people, Matt stood before Chief Justice John Roberts to take the oath of office for the second time. I couldn't stand the formal tension, so I leaned over to the microphone.

"This is the second oath of office you've taken, Mr. President," I said. "Let's make it stick this time."

The crowd laughed and applauded. After the shit we've been through in the past few weeks, I figured some levity was in order.

"...so help me God." Matt said as he finished the oath. The crowd roared.

"Madam Chief of Staff," he said as he turned to me, "it gives me great pleasure to relieve you of your duties as Chief of Staff and to reinstall you as First Lady of the United States of America." More cheers and applause.

I never thought I'd be so relieved to be fired from a position.

"Tony Riordan, you are hereby reinstalled as Chief of Staff to the president—with back pay."

Again the crowd freaked out. These people were starting to look like the home crowd after a winning championship game. I had prepared a list of people that Matt should thank, as well as a list of things for him to do before the daily grind of office took over. I passed the list by Tony Riordan, the man who just succeeded me. Matt turned to Rolly Benton, who stood there with the widest smile I ever saw him wear.

"President Benton, on behalf of myself as well as the people of the United States, I thank you for your outstanding service to your country. I thank you for rescuing me and Tony, and for returning the *USS Louisiana* to its proper owner. And I thank you for keeping Dee busy."

The ceremony broke at 1:15 and lunch was served to a specially invited group at the White House.

"Hey, skinny," I said to Matt, "go for the pasta and the ice cream sundae. You look like a guy who's been in solitary confinement for a few weeks."

"I've been on a strict diet of beets and mashed potatoes," Matt said as he leaned over next to my ear. He knows that breathing into my ear makes me crazy. "For all those weeks I couldn't get you out of my mind. I still can't, so I won't try," Matt said.

Although the festivities were enjoyable, I couldn't wait to get back to the White House where we could be alone. I leaned over and whispered into his ear, just as he had whispered into mine.

"Hey, big guy, let's go home and make love," I said.

He didn't say anything. He reached down under the table and caressed my leg. I reached over and rubbed his.

"How about now?" I said. The crowd was starting to get on my nerves.

"Great idea, hon," he said, "but something tells me it would be inappropriate for the President to stand up with a hard on."

Lunch was winding down, not that the assembled senators and congressmen were running out of things to say for the camera. Tony Riordan walked over to us with an envelope.

"This was just delivered by courier marked 'your eyes only,' Mr. President. It's been through chemical analysis, so you can open it."

Matt opened the envelope and held the letter so I could see it.

"Hello, President Blake:

In keeping with the tradition I set for myself, I won't offer my congratulations, but only an observation. You somehow managed to pull it off again.

Until the next time,
Sincerely,

Bartholomew Martin"

CHARACTERS – *THE PRESIDENT IS MISSING*

Akhbar, Gamal – *See*, Buster
Asidi, Basir – Iranian foreign ministry official
Behzadi, Ali – Iranian Mullah
Baxter, Dwight – Navy Seal Commander
Benton, Roland – Interim President of the United States
Bingham, Walter – Aide to Bartholomew Martin
Buster – CIA agent
Campbell, Joseph – Captain, *USS Louisiana*
Carlini, William – Director, CIA
Chernekov, Boris – New President of Russia
Conklin, Michael – Marine officer stationed aboard the *Louisiana*.
Gillespie, Bill – Commander, *Louisiana*'s weapons officer
Jackson, Phil – Petty Officer and guard over President Blake
Keaton, Wallace – Captain, head of the Office of Naval Intelligence
Patterson, Ashley – Admiral, US Navy, Chief of Naval Operations
Petrov, Boris – Russian submarine captain
Riordan, Tony – Chief of Staff to President Blake
Rouhani, Basim – Iranian Mullah
Spratt, Peter – Commander Submarine Forces, United States Navy
Tavana, Abad – Iranian Mullah, Grand Leader

Townsend, Jack – Attorney for Ludmila and Vasili Yuschenko
Tubin, James – Petty officer on the *Louisiana*.
Yakov, Sergei – Russian Minister of Commerce
Yuschenko, Ludmila – Wife of Admiral Yuschenko
Yuschenko, Vasili – Admiral, Russian Navy
Zhukov, Vladimir – General, Russian Army

ABOUT THE AUTHOR

Russ Moran is the author of *The Gray Ship*, Book One of *The Time Magnet* series. It's a story of time travel, romance, and a nuclear warship that finds itself in the Civil War. *The Thanksgiving Gang* is the sequel. *A Time of Fear* is Book Three, *The Skies of Time* is Book Four in the series, and *The Keepers of Time* is Book Five.

The Shadows of Terror is Book One of *The Patterns Series*, followed by *The Scent of Revenge*.

The President is Missing, is Book Three of the Matt Blake Series. *Sideswiped* and *The Reformers* are Books One and Two of the series.

He has also published five nonfiction books: *Justice in America: How it Works—How it Fails*; *The APT Principle: The Business Plan That You Carry in Your Head*; *Boating Basics: The Boattalk Book of Boating Tips*; *If You're Injured: A Consumer Guide to Personal Injury Law*; *How to Create More Time.* He's a lawyer and a veteran of the United States Navy. He lives on Long Island, New York, with his wife, Lynda.

If you enjoyed *The President is Missing*, please consider leaving a review on amazon.com.

THE BOOKS OF RUSS MORAN

All books are available on Amazon.com, and also on The Kindle.

The Gray Ship – Book One of *The Time Magnet Series*
http://amzn.to/16GPumH

"This provocative, intensely powerful novel is a must-read for sci-fi fans and Civil War aficionados, though mainstream fiction readers will find it heart-rending and inspiring as well. A rare read that's not only wildly entertaining, but also profoundly moving."

— Kirkus Reviews

The Thanksgiving Gang – Book Two of *The Time Magnet Series* http://amzn.to/1NzBs7N

"I had never read a book before written in an efficient, minimalistic prose... Instead of writing what most readers want to read, he gives voice to life-like characters, with their flaws and prejudices. They are not infallible superheroes. It's always nice to find a new voice in fiction and to enjoy creativity at its best."

— C. Ludewig

A Time of Fear – Book Three of *The Time Magnet Series*
http://amzn.to/1zdjaG9

"His story is fascinating, and adds even more depth to this already cavernously deep novel. Amazingly unique, chilling and well written, Moran weaves a future that is both desperate and hopeful. Blending modern fears with science fiction results in a tale that will keep you reading long into the night." Five stars!"

—Heather

The Skies of Time – Book Four of *The Time Magnet Series*
http://amzn.to/1CCC3jg

In *The Skies of Time*, you will recognize the two main characters, Ashley Patterson, now an admiral, and her husband, Jack Thurber. They met and fell in love in *The Gray Ship*, and now they're in for the adventure of their lives in *The Skies of Time*. Ashley and Jack have been such prominent characters in all four books of The Time Magnet Series that I feel like they're old friends. You will also recognize some of the other characters. But if I told you who they are, it would ruin the fun.

"I'm big fan of this series and this one may be the best. I hope there is another book to this series since it keeps getting better. There is a few questions I have about certain events that makes the next one even more suspenseful. These are great books to binge read one after the other."

— Time Travel Fan

The Shadows of Terror – Book One of the *Patterns Series*
http://amzn.to/1IDQzJS
A novel that explodes off the front page of your newspaper.

Terrorism now has a new face, a face that's obscured in the shadows. The radical forces of destruction have learned to make themselves invisible to the West, and preventing a terrorist attack has become almost impossible.

A new war has begun, World War III.

Rick Bellamy, an FBI agent who specializes in counterterrorism, is engaged in his own war, a war with no end.

Bellamy's wife, Ellen, a prominent architect, discovers that she's in the middle of the greatest terror plot to date.

To defeat the enemy, Bellamy first has to uncover the clues, to shine a light on the shadows. He has to find patterns – before it's too late.

"Move over James Patterson and Mary Higgins Clark. There's a new guy in town. Russ Moran's new book – *The Shadows of Terror.*"

— Frank from Lynbrook

The Scent of Revenge, - Book Two in the *Patterns Series.*
http://amzn.to/1UvDRmw

The world is at war – World War III. FBI Agent Rick Bellamy and his wife, Ellen, find themselves in the middle of a sinister terror plot.

Someone is attacking young prominent women, inflicting a horrible disease.

Nobody knows its origin, nobody knows how to stop it, nobody knows how to cure it.

Rick Bellamy and a team of scientists want to go on offense. But how?

Will the lives of the women be changed forever? When will the attacks stop?

"Heart pounding, can't put down thriller that will force you to look at terrorism in different light. Life in America will never be the same."

—Cold Coffee Cafe

Sideswiped - Book One in the Matt Blake series of legal thrillers.
http://amzn.to/1MkxX35
Trial lawyer Matt Blake took on a perfect case.

It involved a sideswipe collision in which his client's husband, an investigative reporter, was killed. The evidence of negligence was overwhelming. Eyewitnesses testified that defendant was talking on his cell phone when he hit the other car.

But was it negligence? Was it an accident?

Or was it murder?

Matt uncovers evidence that the act may have been intentional. Somebody wanted the man dead. Somebody wanted the man silenced.

Somebody had a lot to hide.

The signs started to point to the highest levels of government.

An open-and-shut personal injury case suddenly became a vast conspiracy of terror.

"This books hooks you in from the first line. You are drawn into the world of Matt Blake and become emotionally attached to him and his journey. The story itself is so well-written and moves quickly so there is never a dull moment."

—Sarah Elle

I love Book 1 in this new series!

By Russell Moran demonstrates the depth of his writing talent by developing a new genre with *Sideswiped*. Branching out from his previous novels dealing with time travel, Moran goes in a whole new direction with Book One in the Matt Blake series. He creates a wild but totally believable story of modern day intrigue and suspense.

Moran also deftly weaves into this book some of my favorite characters from his prior novels. I am looking forward to starting Book #2 - *The Reformers* — Frank from Lynbrook on August 16, 2016

The Reformers - Book Two of the Matt Blake series of legal thrillers, the sequel to *Sideswiped*.
http://amzn.to/2m8uMdu

The forces of radical Islam are on the run.

Their leadership has been decimated, their ranks thinned, their power disappearing by the week.

Their recruiting efforts have been cut off, the radical websites shut down, and the attraction of jihad is losing its appeal among the young.

With targeted assassinations, military strikes, as well as the loss of oil fields and gold mines, radical Islam is fast losing power.

But who is responsible?

It isn't the United States Government. It's a new force the world has never seen before.

Lawyer Matt Blake and his wife Diana find themselves in the middle of the most gigantic plot the world has ever seen, a conspiracy that's only begun to grow.

"I've been a fan of the author, Russell Moran, since reading *Sideswiped* a few months ago, so I admittedly went into this book with quite high expectations. That being said, I had no idea that "*The Reformers*" was going to play out in the way that it does and I can see myself giving this book a re-read in the future. In fact, I am even more impressed by the storyline of this read than the last and it has left me excited to see more."

Lucidity.

The President is Missing, the book you've just read, is Book Three of the Matt Blake Series.

If you enjoyed *The President is Missing,* please consider leaving a brief review on amazon.com